The Country Club

C. ATKINSON

Copyright © 2022 C. Atkinson.

ALL RIGHTS RESERVED. This book contains material protected under International and Federal Copyright Laws and Treaties. Any unauthorized reprint or use of this material is prohibited. No part of this book may be reproduced or transmitted in any form or by any means, electronic or mechanical, including photocopying, recording, or by any information storage and retrieval system without writtenpermission from the author/publisher.

This is a work of fiction. Names, characters, places, and incidents either are a product of the author's imagination or are used fictitiously. Any resemblance to actual persons, living or dead, events or locales is entirely coincidental.

ISBN: 978-1-64184-816-9 (Paperback)
ISBN: 978-1-64184-818-3 (Ebook)

...a Build Series novel

Dedication

To my mom, Boots Chopnak,
who loved to play golf.
May 12, 1936 - August 27, 2021

Chapter 1

"So, let's get started. I'm Dick Buzzy, General Manager of Golden Gate City and Country Club. This is the first construction committee meeting for the renovation of the Country Clubhouse. The club was established in 1860 and is the oldest athletic club in the United States. Originally built in 1922, the Country Clubhouse has undergone decades of expansion and improvement and is in dire need of the next one. H&S, the general contractor for the project, is also here to answer any questions you might have. Why don't we just go around the table and introduce yourselves, your organization, and include your involvement on the project."

Pointing, Dick motions to start left to right.

"Hi, I'm Dick Blue. I am the retired president of Blue Construction. I've been a club member and in the construction industry for thirty years. I thought I could add my experience with the club and in the industry to the project."

Sounds pretty solid to me.

"Dick Molanari here. I am a retired managing partner of Anderson Architects. I would like to see this clubhouse shine again and want to be a part of the project."

"Hi. I am the architect of this project. I work for Renovation Architects. My name is Dick Leggett. Next."

"It's a pleasure to meet everyone. I'm Loretta Novak. I will be the project manager on this project for H&S, the general contractor."

"Dick Stone, engineer of record, a principal of Stone Engineering. The structural elements of this project might make all of us sleep less at night, but in the end, it will be fabulous!"

I am impressed with him already.

"I'm Dick Jones, Country Club Manager here at the Golden Gate Club."

"Hey, Dick Little here. I am a private consultant and have been selected by the committee to be the construction manager and consultant for this project."

Can you imagine going through life with that name!

"I also have been in the construction industry and a member of the club for twenty-five years," he adds.

Let's just hope he got this job on merit, not favors.

"Our role on this project is to give all the contractors and consultants adequate guidance and make decisions needed to get this job done. We need to stand together as a team, giving clear direction and decisions about the project. We need no politics, no attitudes, and no agendas. Members may approach you and ask you favors or request you sway decisions in their direction, but I will not allow that. Our team should not allow that. We will meet on the last Tuesday of the month at 10 a.m. in the temporary clubhouse. Dick Jones, the clubhouse manager, will keep minutes for our meetings and distribute them to you every month."

"We can start questions." Dick Buzzy instructs.

"Loretta, so what do you do when a conflict arises between you and a subcontractor?" asks Dick Blue.

"For Christ's sake, Dick, she's from Pittsburgh. She won't have any problems," Dick Molanari pipes in.

"What about the areas of the clubhouse that don't allow women, including our project manager?" Dick Leggett questions.

"I'll work with Dick Jones to figure that one out," says Dick Buzzy.

Sounds like they don't have a clue what to do with me.

"Do you play golf?" Dick Buzzy questions. Before I get a chance to answer, Dick Stone blasts out, "I've played golf with her, and she hits the ball a ton."

He didn't say I was a good golfer, just that I hit the ball a ton. That could mean "long and wrong."

As they continue to ask and answer all their questions themselves, Dick Buzzy finally says, "Thanks, Loretta. We will send a contract to H&S to review. I'm sure we can come to an agreement. Welcome aboard."

"Thank you," I say as I sneak out the door with a smile and a wave.

It's such a guy thing to do to jump in and answer a question for me before I've had a chance to respond. *Only to help me out, I'm sure.* The management by committee syndrome has already started. They, the committee members, all think they are in charge, but no one has the authority to do anything. They all think they're right, and they all like to make sure everyone hears what they have to say.

I head back to the H&S main office in the city. After my project at 333 Folsom shut down, I got an office on the executive floor. It was the only office available. It should only be a few weeks until we start the job, and I can move to the country club. I walk into my office, and there is the most beautiful arrangement of fresh flowers, forty-eight tulips in an assortment of colors, spanning three feet in diameter.

Wow! I have never seen anything like this.

I sit down on the front edge of my desk, staring at this masterpiece, and I can feel there are others present. Looking to the doorway, I see three gals, executive secretaries, who are dying to find out who my Prince Charming is. I smile at them and slowly shake my head. They slowly turn and walk single file out of my office, all with disappointing looks on their faces. I'm sure they thought I'd be very excited to share the contents of the attached card, but I have learned that sharing is a no-no, especially with office employees.

Finally, I sit down at my desk, and the phone rings. "Hi, this is Loretta."

"Hi, this is Carroll."

"Oh my God, how are you?" I ask.

"I'm fine. Just calling to see if you can meet with me tomorrow if that's possible." "Sure, what's it about?"

"I think you know what it's about. Meet me on the top floor of 250 Montgomery at 10 a.m."

"Okay, Carroll," I say. "I'll be there."

As I hang up the phone, I try to remember which Dick works for what company and which Dick has what role on the project. *They're all named DICK!* I remember a party that I went to once, and it seemed like all the guys were named Steve, but I've never been on a project team where everyone on the committee was named Dick. I'm the only one not named Dick. I'm the only female on the project.

I sit at my desk and think I may have to give the Dicks nicknames, so I can remember who is who.

Dick Buzzy is easy. I'll call him Buzz.

I think I'll keep Dick Little as Dick Little.

Dick Leggett, the architect, will be Dick the architect. Dick Stone, the engineer, will be Dick the engineer.

Dick Molanari and Dick Blue will just be Dick. The chances of either of them answering if I called them Dick is pretty good.

Gosh, this is like playing town and country in the basement when I was five, with my Lego buildings and my Matchbox cars. I would come up with names for everyone who lived in the town. I would give them vehicles that would match their imaginary names and jobs that matched their vehicles; whether it be a tow truck or a convertible, their names had to fit.

Real life isn't much different. My friends and family give nicknames to their friends and family all the time. Like Lolly, my nickname.

Nicknames are often a shortened version of the person's last name, like Phil, for Philip, Chop, for

Chopnak, and Woz, for Wozniak. Sometimes nicknames refer to the person's physical attributes, such as Shorty, Big Mike, or Tiny. Nicknames can also represent what the person is passionate about, such as Bobby Baseball, Post Office Jimmy, or Tan Dan.

These nicknames are never meant to be offensive, prejudiced, or racist. These names are friendly and affectionate. It's all in fun.

Chapter 2

I go to the office in the morning and work for about an hour before I leave to meet Carroll at 250 Montgomery. I haven't seen Carroll since the day his mother died. I thought I would never see him again. That's what happens to clients. You spend all this time with them while you're building the project and then never see them again when the project is complete. That's why they told me the most important thing I could do as a project manager is develop a relationship with the client. *I did that and look where it got me.*

I leave the office and walk down California Street and turn right on Montgomery. I walk into the lobby of 250 Montgomery and call the elevator. I hear the bell, the doors open. I walk in and push the 21st floor. As I travel up, I think about not knowing what this meeting is about, although Carroll seems to think I know.

The elevator doors open on floor twenty-one, and I step out. I see a large table with Carroll, the sole occupant. He looks and smiles. I walk over to him and give him a big hug.

"Do you want a coffee?"

"Yes, please," I say.

I haven't been in this room before. It is all windows, with a beautiful view, a huge wooden table in the middle of the room, and twelve chairs. It must be the board room.

Carroll returns with my coffee, sits down, and looks at me. "You look great. What have you been doing?" I ask.

"We are not here to talk about me. We are here to talk about you. So, what the hell do you think you're doing?" Carroll asks, as my eyes grow wide and my heart shrinks.

"I didn't do anything."

I feel like I am sixteen again, and my father just caught me necking with a boy in front of the house. "I didn't do anything!" was always my reply.

"I haven't seen Ben since we had breakfast three weeks ago."

"Well, that's good," Carroll replies. "I'm just trying to shed some light on the proposition at hand, assuming it's still a proposition and not a reality."

"I'll say it again. I didn't do anything."

"If that's the case," Carroll says, "I still have an opportunity to give you my advice. Ben is a rich man and comes from a rich family. He can be very persuasive with money. On the other hand, you work from paycheck to paycheck for a construction company. It seems to me you might be persuaded by money. Ben is the type that makes sure he gets what he wants, and for some ungodly reason, he wants you."

I'm not sure how to take Carroll's words. Does he mean he doesn't think I'm good enough for Ben, or does he think it's wrong for Ben to want me?

"Carroll, I appreciate the advice, but I haven't decided what to do," I explain.

"What do you mean you haven't decided what to do? He's married, for Christ's sake, and he has a kid, and you're still trying to figure it out? That's why we're here. Ben is going to give you everything he can to convince you to have an affair with him because that's what he's decided he wants. And I'm just saying be careful and understand what you are getting yourself into," Carroll says. "I like you, Loretta, but obviously Ben likes you more."

I'm stuck in traffic on the way home. Normally, a half-hour drive takes over an hour in traffic. I pull off the side of the road at Trisha Wilder's house. She lives three doors up from mine in East Marin. Trisha and I sail together, and she is one of my few friends outside of H&S. Trisha grew up in Palo Alto, and as soon as I met her, I knew I would spend time with her. I've spent Thanksgiving and Christmas with her and her family. She'd never let me be alone for the holidays. We raced sailboats to Catalina and have gone to the beach with friends in Southern California. But it's nice to have someone and somewhere to just stop by and say hi, instead of going home to an empty apartment.

I get out of the car, and Trisha is smoking a cigarette on the porch.

"Hey, T," I say. T is my nickname for her.

"How are you? Do you want a glass of wine?" T asks. "Sounds great," I answer and smile.

The views from T's apartment are spectacular. They include three bridges and the last place to get fog on the entire bay. Chris Isaak is on the stereo, and T opens the bottle of wine. T works for her father in Silicon Valley. His business, Wilder Inc., supplies pieces and parts to the electronic and tech industry.

We sit inside at the window, staring at the view, while T pours the wine.

"So, how was your day at Spacely Sprockets?" I ask. Spacely Sprockets is my nickname for Wilder, Inc.

"Don't ask," T responds. "My father fell and will be out of the office for a few weeks.

He wants me to be in the office while he's out. I'm used to being in the field, selling." "I'm sorry, T, about your dad and about your job."

"You and me both. How was your day?" T asks.

"Crazy. I had my first committee meeting for my new project, and the names of all the members of the committee are named Dick!"

"WHAT?"

"I'm serious. I gave some of them nicknames so I can decipher who is who. So, are you in the office for the next few weeks?" I ask.

"I don't think I have a choice. I will be okay. It's only a few weeks," T says.

Chapter 3

"Hi, this is Loretta."

"Hi, Tiger." That's Ben's nickname for me.

"Hi, Ben, how are you?" Loretta asks.

I have been waiting for this phone call for three weeks, and I still haven't figured out what I'm going to say to him.

"I'm fine. I want to know if you can have lunch with me tomorrow?" Ben asks. "Umm. I can't."

"What do you mean you can't?" Ben wonders. "I mean, I can't go tomorrow."

"Why not?" Ben questions.

"I have an outpatient surgery at SF Med. I can't drive there or home, so I don't know what I'm going to do. I can ask T, but she has to work."

"It's not a problem. I'll have Bo pick you up at your apartment, and Drew can drive you home! What time is your appointment?" Ben asks.

"Ten a.m. I have to be there by 9 a.m. They said I'd be ready to go home by 2 p.m."

"I'll take care of it for you. You don't have to worry," Ben states.

I've heard this before.

"You don't have to do this. I can figure it out on my own," I say.

"No, it's all taken care of, Tiger."

"Call me and let me know your address so Bo knows where he's going to pick you up at 8 a.m."

"Can't I just tell you my address right now?" I ask.
"Yes, that would be easier."

"550 Viewpoint Drive, East Marin. Thank you so much. I really didn't know what to do," I admit.

I can almost see Ben smiling over the phone because he knows he can help me. I am going in for a female procedure called a colposcopy, which removes a part of the cervix that has weird cells. No one said I have cancer, just weird cells.

The next day at 8 a.m., this huge white limo pulls up in front of my triplex. I'm surprised the neighbors didn't all run out into the street in their pajamas, assuming Chris Issac or Seal would stumble out of the vehicle.

This is not a limo kind of neighborhood.

Bo parks and makes his way up ten steps. I open the door before he knocks, with a travel bag in hand. My mouth drops at the site of the white limo.

"Hi, I'm Loretta," I say. "Bo. Nice to meet you."
"Thanks for helping me out today."
"Not a problem, ma'am. My pleasure," Bo says.

Bo is a tall, buff guy with dark hair and a tan. He's very good-looking. By the time we got into the limo and back on the road, we went right past T's house. She was getting in her car and going to work herself.

I saw her stare as we drove past. The dark windows would never reveal who was inside, so she'll probably spend all day guessing who it was.

As we pull up at the hospital, there is a nurse with a wheelchair waiting at the curb. Bo gets out and walks around to the back to let me out. At this point, the nurse looks like she is anticipating Chris Issac or Seal to get out. Bo opens the door, and I pop out. The nurse looks very disappointed that it is only me.

"Thanks, Bo." I smile.

"You're welcome, Miss Loretta."

I open my eyes in the recovery room, and Drew is standing next to my bed—eyelashes and all. He'd make any recovery go quickly.

"Hi Loretta," Drew says softly. "Hi. Thanks for helping me." "My pleasure." Drew smiles.

Fifteen minutes later, we are on our way. Drew started working for Ben about a month ago and has the job that I wanted. *Perfect*.

"So, how's your new job?" I ask

"I love it. Ben teaches me everything I need to know to do the job, and I'm getting the hang of it pretty quickly," Drew says.

"So do you remember the meeting Ben and I had the last day we were at the job site?" I ask Drew.

"Yes. I told you he was probably going to offer you a job," Drew says. "I guess I was wrong."

"Do you know what he did ask me?" "No."

"He wants to have an affair with me," I announce.

"WHAT?" Drew blasts. "I went to dinner with him and his wife last week!"

"And?"

"And what?" Drew asks.

"I'm just trying to figure it out," I say.

I tell Drew the exit to take to get to my triplex. He's able to park easier than the limo. He grabs my arm to help me out of the car and helps me up the steps. I unlock the door and open it. Drew follows me.

"Wow, what a view!" he screams.

"Yeah, I like living here. Thanks again for helping me today. It was good to see you."

I turn and give him a hug, briefly, and he smiles. He turns and walks out the door.

Chapter 4

Two days later, I am back at work after a day of rest, more from the anesthesia than the procedure itself. I received the contract from the club. It stated the job start is February 1st. The completion date is November 8th because November 10th is the father-daughter dinner dance, and the schedule revolves entirely around that one occasion. The dance is an annual event.

Today is January 29th, and according to Bill, the H&S superintendent, they are nowhere near moved out of that clubhouse. Where they are running behind is moving the members out of the men's locker room, but that's just what I have been told. I have never seen the space because I'm not allowed in it. The locker room was renovated in the 1950s and is more like a bunch of cabanas than a locker room. There are six members per cabana. Guys brought their La-Z-Boys, card tables, and mini-refrigerators for their little private areas.

From what I understand, the members are responsible for moving their personal belongings out of their cabanas by January 31st so that construction can start on February 1st. The club is also responsible for setting up a few double-wide, temporary trailers in the parking lot to house the restaurant, one meeting room, and the manager's office. They are just a few days behind in running temporary power and phone, installing a small commercial kitchen, and moving the dining furniture and wares to the trailers.

The second committee meeting is on January 30th in the meeting room in the temporary clubhouse. There's no heat yet, but the power and lights work.

I walk in right at the start of the meeting. All the Dicks are here. Dick Buzzy kicks things off.

"Welcome. Yesterday, a building inspector was here. He made it perfectly clear that all occupants had to be out of the building before H&S can mobilize and start demolition," Buzz states.

"Screw the building inspector. Why was he here anyway?" asks Dick Little.

"H&S pulled a building permit a month ago, so they know a project is beginning.

We need to develop a relationship with this inspector to get through this project," I say.

I don't like this guy's attitude!

"Who is still here?" Dick asks.

"Well, there are residents on the second floor." *What second floor?* "We thought they could stay, but obviously, I'm wrong, D." That's Buzz's nickname for Dick Jones. "Can you talk to the renters and kindly ask them to vacate?" Buzz asks.

I'm told there are "rooms upstairs," which sounds creepy, that primarily are used when someone gets kicked out of their home and has nowhere else to go. It's only temporary, supposedly, until they find a place or go back home.

"Sure," D says, "but it can't happen by tomorrow."

"Then H&S can't mobilize and start construction by February 1st," I pipe up. "This will be a day-to-day delay until we are clear to start."

"No, it won't!" Dick Little screams. "This will not delay the project."

"Sorry, but this is the most obvious delay," I state. "If you delay the start, you delay the finish. Unless you delete or change some of the work, this will cause a delay, and I don't think anyone on the committee will agree to delete work to maintain the schedule. I can't hold to a November 8th completion, not knowing when we will start."

"But you have to," Dick says, "because the father-daughter dance is on November 10th, come hell or high water."

Chapter 5

We are not going anywhere fast with this project. I'm still in the office, on the executive floor, biding my time until H&S gets released to move to the job site. It's quarter past four, and the phone rings.

"Hi, this is Loretta." "Hi, this is Ben."

Silence on my part because I couldn't think of anything to say. "Do you have time for a drink tonight?" Ben asks.

"I think so. I'm in the office in the financial district. Where are you?" I ask. "In my office. I can meet you at Jerry's on Bush in fifteen minutes," Ben says.

"See you then," I say.

Oh my, what did I get myself into? This will be the first time I have seen Ben since our infamous breakfast, and I am not sure what to even say to him. I pack my office up and head over to Jerry's. I hope to be the first one there. When I walk in, I see Ben sitting at the bar, smiling at me. I walk over and stop in front of him. Ben stands and gives me the biggest bear hug and a kiss on the cheek. I sit on the stool next to him and order a glass of zinfandel. Ben takes a sip of his Absolut. I settle myself and look at him.

I'm still not turned on by this guy. Who knows why?

"So, did Bo take care of you last week?" Ben asks. "It was fun riding around in the limo." I smile. "That's my car to commute in," Ben states.

"Really!" I say. Maybe I didn't get a sense of wealth from him on our last project. "And Drew took care of me as well. He loved my triplex. It was good to see him," I say.

"Hopefully, I will get to see what Drew was all excited about at your triplex," Ben mentions. "Drew is doing a great job. I'm glad I hired him."

"I'm glad you hired him too." *And what about hiring me?*

Ben orders another round for us and then asks, "So, what is your next project?"

"The Golden Gate Country Club restoration," I state.

"Wow. I didn't think they let women in there."
"They don't," I say, "except for Sunday brunch."

As I watch Ben close out the tab, I notice he is wearing cufflinks. "Say, I just noticed your cufflinks. I don't think I recognized them before."

"I usually wore golf shirts to the job site, not dress shirts. All my dress shirts have cufflink holes. I have quite a collection of them," Ben says.

"It's very sophisticated," I proclaim. "Or should I say formal."

Nothing about construction is formal.

I look at the time and say, "Wow. I really must go. It was great seeing you."

"So, what about us?" Ben asks.

Oh, no. I knew he'd ask. I'm sure he knows I met with Carroll, and I'm sure he has a plan for "us." I'm still not ready to buy into it.

"I'm not sure about 'us' yet, Ben," I explain.

"If you need more time, I understand," Ben says. As he is talking, he pulls out a plastic bag that has diamond earrings in it. "I want you to have these."

"I don't know what to say."

"You don't have to say anything," Ben says. "Just put them on."

I pull them from the plastic bag and put them in my ears. I try to smile. "Thank you. They are beautiful," I say. "I got to run."

I pull in front of T's house once I get to East Marin and walk in the front. It's windy outside, so she is inside, looking at the view.

"Hey T, how are you?"

I think I startle her because she jumps up, almost spilling her wine. "Hi, Lolly. Come on in."

She goes for a wine glass for me and fills both up as we sit down at the window.

"So, what's new?" T asks.

"Well, I went out for drinks with Ben today. He asked if I thought about the affair, and I told him I still needed some time. At that point, he pulled out a plastic bag with one-carat diamond earrings for me," I explain.

"WHAT?" T screams. She looks at me and checks out my new earrings. "Nice."

"I'm not too sure what to think anymore. Drew told me he had dinner with Ben and his wife last week. Maybe that's why men want to have affairs instead of business relationships with women, to include their wives and business associates in dinner, but not their mistresses."

"I wonder what kind of gifts he gives his wife if he gives you diamond earrings," T wondered.

"Good question, but I don't care. I don't care about his wife. In fact, I feel sorry for his wife. You have to wonder if she knows about the affairs he has had. I have a feeling having affairs is just something he does."

Chapter 6

After a trip to the gynecologist, I was told I needed another colposcopy…that they didn't "get" it all. I'm not sure about any of this. I have a funny suspicion that they like my insurance company. They got paid the first time, so why not try it again. Since I've done this before, I think only one day off will be necessary. But I do need an escort to and from the hospital.

I call Ben.

"Hi, this is Ben."

"Hi, this is Loretta. I need a favor. I'm scheduled to have another outpatient procedure on Tuesday, and I need some transportation again," I say.

"Not a problem. I'll have Bo pick you up from home tomorrow, and he'll pick you up from the hospital as well," Ben says. "But bring some clothes for a few days."

"Why?" I ask.

"We're going to New York after I pick you up from the hospital."

I pack some New York outfits *like I know what New York outfits are* and think, *What on earth are we doing in New York?* I didn't commit to an affair, and I hope this trip doesn't make me commit to an affair. I'll have to wait and see.

I wake up from the anesthesia and see Ben standing there. "Hi," I say. "They said it would be fifteen minutes before I can leave."

"Are you OK?" Ben asks. "Yes, I'm fine."

Twenty minutes later, we are in the limo, heading for SFO.

"So, do you have business in New York?" I ask.

"Yes, but only for four hours. The rest of the time, we can explore the city."

Our flight is on time, and we board first. First class. I never flew first class before. I relax in a big seat that is wide and comfortable. There is a cocktail and snack served to you before you take off while everyone else is boarding.

I'm still a little groggy from the procedure and fall asleep as soon as we're in the air. Ben is working. It's a five-hour flight, and I wake up with less than thirty minutes to go. Ben looks at me and smiles. I feel fine but still groggy.

A town car picks us up at the airport and takes us to the Four Seasons Hotel in Manhattan. We check in and have the luggage delivered to the room. Suite, I mean. We walk into a fabulous suite with a fruit, cheese, and wine basket waiting for us. And a bottle of Absolut. I still don't feel all that great, so I lay down on the couch and wait for the luggage to arrive. Ben has been on the phone constantly since we got here.

I'm not even sure what I'm doing here.

When the luggage arrives, I am shown to my room in the suite. It is an enormous space with a view of Broadway. All three bedrooms are just as huge. Dinner is ordered and delivered to the room, and I'm glad we're not going out. Ben has a meeting tomorrow morning, and I can recover from the travel and everything else all morning.

Ben's meeting is at 8 a.m. His breakfast arrived at 7 a.m. I was still asleep with the time change. I woke up at 8:30 a.m., and I'm thinking it's 5:30 a.m. I order breakfast and just enjoy the view above the busy New York streets while I wait for room service. Once my breakfast arrives, I cuddle into a dining room table chair and am served by the staff. Boy, this is hard to get used to.

Ben shows back up at the suite at 11:30 a.m. "Hi," he says. "How do you feel?" "I'm fine. This place is very nice. Thank you for bringing me here."

"Are you ready to go sightseeing?" Ben asks. "We can go to lunch, the museums, whatever you would like."

Since I'm still trying to figure out what I'm doing here, I may as well enjoy myself. "How about lunch?" I choose.

"I know exactly the place we'll go," Ben says. "Are you ready?" "Yes. Is it cold outside?" I ask.

"Wear something warm, just in case," Ben states.

We make our way through the hotel lobby, out to the sidewalk, and around the corner to the Plaza Hotel. Across the street, there are horse-drawn carriages to take you into Central Park. We cross the street and board a carriage.

"Tavern on the Green, please," Ben requests. "No problem," the driver says.

We start making our way into the park. There are many people that utilize this park. Joggers, walkers, bench sitters, dog walkers, you name it. They are here.

Our carriage takes us through the beautiful parts of the park. We finally arrive at the restaurant. We get off the carriage and enter the restaurant. What a fabulous place this is. We have an amazing lunch, and the carriage comes back for us. We start into the park again, but this time it's a different route. Wow. Really nice. By the time we get back to the Plaza Hotel, we are ready for a cocktail. We walk back to the Four Seasons and head for our suite.

We open the basket and set out some cheese and crackers, I mix an Absolut over with an olive for Ben, and I open a bottle of Zinfandel and pour myself a glass.

"So, did you enjoy yourself today?" Ben asks.

"It was incredible. This is the first time I've ever been to New York City. It's pretty impressive." I smile. "I'm going to call T to let her know I'm OK."

"That's fine," Ben says and walks off to give me some privacy.

I call T's phone. I don't even know if she's home from work yet. The phone rings a few times.

"Hello?" T says.

"Hi, it's Lolly. I'm calling to tell you that I'm fine and in New York City."

"WHAT? New York City?" she screams. "I wondered where you were. You haven't stopped by in a few days," T says.

"Well, I had a second colposcopy, and Ben picked me up from the hospital, and we went right to the airport. I was pretty groggy, and I slept most of the flight. I'll stop by when I get home, which will be tomorrow evening."

"Thanks for checking in, and any time tomorrow before 9 p.m. works for me," T says.

Ben comes out to fix another cocktail, and he sees I'm off the phone. He sits down next to me, and I smile at him.

"So, have you thought any more about us?" Ben asks.

I knew he was going to go there. I just didn't know when. "Jury's still out on this one, Ben. Oh, and by the way, the doctor said no sex for six weeks, so nothing is happening in New York City."

It's late, but it feels like it's early, so we order room service and make it an early evening.

In the morning, we pack our bags, grab a coffee to go, and head straight for the Metropolitan Museum of Art in the town car. Our flight leaves at 1:30 p.m., so we don't have much time. This museum is stunning. I've never seen anything like it. We make our way around the first floor and decide it's time to go to the airport. It's a shame. It could take days to meander around this place. We board the plane. First-class seating is nice. Food, drinks, and big chairs. Five hours later, we are in San Francisco.

"Thanks, Ben. What a great trip," I say as I give him a big hug. "I'll be in touch." Ben smiles.

Bo puts me and my luggage in the limo. Forty-five minutes later, we are in East Marin. I can't believe I'm home and it's only six o'clock. I get up the steps, with Bo carrying my luggage, and unlock the door. We both walk in.

He turns and says, "Is there anything else I can do for you?"

"Yes, as a matter of fact. Can you ride me to the neighbor's house, three doors up?" I ask.

"Certainly. Are you ready to go now?" Bo asks.

"Yes," I say.

We're back in the limo and make it to T's house.

"Thanks, Bo." I smile.

"You're welcome."

As I get out of the limo, I see T walk out of her front door. I walk up to her, and she says, "WHAT?" I give her a big hug. I'm just glad to be home.

"So, it's you who I've seen driving up the road in the limo!" T announces. We walk into her house, and I sit down to relax. It's been a long day.

"I'll tell you all about it. Have any wine open?" I ask. "Yes, red or white?"

"Red, please."

I sit at the window, looking at the view of San Francisco. T brings our wine over. "So, you went to New York City?" T asks.

"Yes, it was pretty spectacular." "What is he up to?" T asks.

"I'm not sure. I'm not sleeping with him, and he doesn't seem to mind."

Maybe I should worry about that.

"We stayed in a suite in the Four Seasons, got a horse-drawn carriage to Tavern on the Green for lunch, went to the Metropolitan Museum of Art. It was unbelievable," I explain.

"He didn't give you any more diamonds, did he?" T asks.

"No, the trip was enough. I'm sure he's trying to get me to fall for him," I conclude.

"Well, are you?"

Chapter 7

It's February 15th, and H&S is finally moving into their job-site office. The committee chose the president's room for the contractor's office because it has a separate entry, close to the blue rooms, my nickname for outhouses, and only is scheduled for new paint and carpet. H&S will be able to stay in their office for 98 percent of the construction.

The clubhouse is Spanish-style architecture, with a clay tile roof and stucco exterior. The roadway into the club has a driveway to the left that goes in front of the clubhouse. It is circular, around a bed of flowers. The area is very well kept by the clubhouse landscape crew and is quite beautiful, especially for a job site.

The pro shop is not getting renovated and is just 800 feet up the hill from the clubhouse. The temporary facilities for the members are up and running. It is a little odd for the client to be in the double wides and the contractor in the clubhouse. Since all occupants have vacated and the building inspector has given us the green light to move in and start construction, I can roam the joint at my leisure—the men's bar, the men's locker room, and the second-floor rooms, all the places women aren'tallowed.

The men's locker room is just as it was described to me. Lots of stuff was left there, and the demo contractor will get it out of there with everything else. I know the members are feeling devastated. Remember when you built a couch cave with all the couch cushions? You put all your stuff and toys in it, and it was perfect. Then, Mom came home and told you to clean all this shit up because Dad was on his way home, and you were devastated. Yeah, that feeling.

The demolition contractor has an ingenious way of tackling this project. They cut a hole in the exterior of the building, large enough to drive a small front loader in and out of the building. They use the equipment to pull down the interior stuff, pick it up, and haul it out and up the hill to the dumpster. Some of the members stand and watch to see if they can see any of their stuff—*memories*—getting hauled away.

The routine has set in. Contractors have a designated area to park down below the clubhouse. As soon as I drive the Miata in and park, a landscape worker comes over, picks me up, and drives me up to the clubhouse.

"Thank you," I say as I get out of the cart.

He smiles and drives away. I wonder if he speaks English.

I spend a lot of time walking around the site, making mental notes about what used to be there, so I can defend H&S if and when we screw up. Today, I notice that all the exterior light fixtures are gone. I don't know how secure this place is at night, but I do know that people probably know this clubhouse is vacant, and there might be vandalism.

I went back to the office. Bill is there. Bill is the concrete superintendent from my last project. And he's a great concrete super. I just don't know how good he is as an interior finishes superintendent.

"Hi, Bill." "Hi, Loretta."

"I was just walking around the site, and I think someone stole all the exterior light fixtures! They're gone!" I gasp.

"I did," Bill admits. "WHAT?"

"I took them home to restore them and sell them," Bill says excitedly.

"Bill, have you looked at the plans that note 'all existing exterior lighting get renovated by the electrician'?"

Bill looks at me like the cat that just ate the mouse. "I didn't know. I'll bring them back tomorrow."

"Good."

He is making me think he hasn't looked at the blueprints at all. Blueprints are the instructions for the project, the basis of our work in the contract.

Bill brought back the exterior lights that were picked up by the electrician. Demolition is moving on at a fast pace. I sit at my desk in the job office, trying to take care of minor change orders and our pay application for the month.

I look up and see Bill staring at me. "Hi, Loretta," Bill says.

"Hi, Bill. What's going on?" I ask.

"I removed the marble toilet partitions in the main floor restroom, and I sold them," Bill explains.

"To whom?"

"That's not important, but what is important is this." He hands me an envelope.

"What's this?"

"Well, this is $750.00 for marble partitions. It's your party fund."

"I don't know what to say."

"No need to say anything. It's your money now."

Then, I look up as Buzz walks in. "Hi, do you have a minute to walk with me?" "Sure," I say, as I grab my hard hat.

"Do you have a hard hat?" "No," Buzz says.

"I'll get you one."

We walk across the main clubhouse to the kitchen. All the kitchen equipment has been removed, and it's a big space.

"Oh my!" I scream, as I look at the concrete slab. I can see the men's locker room below through the spalling of the slab.

Buzz looks at me. He knows this must be repaired. He knows it will be expensive and may delay the job.

"I'll talk to the Dicks to see what needs to be done. We can talk about it at the committee meeting on Tuesday," Buzz says.

"We just have to move quickly. After the last delay conversation with Dick Little, I'm not looking forward to the next one!"

Today, they are installing the shoring in the existing building to support the building below. I reserved the circle for the activity. The steel beam for the shoring arrives on-site on a flatbed 18-wheeler. The crane pulls in shortly after. The crane hoists the beam into the existing structure. Bill and I watched them install the shoring, holding our breath. A crowd gathered around us on the driveway to watch as well. When the crane pulls back, we all clap. Now that it is in place, excavation can start on the front of the building, and the existing structure will literally hang from the shoring. *I think this is what Dick the engineer said would keep us up at night.*

The committee meeting is held in the conference room of the double wides. All the Dicks are here.

"Hi, everyone," Buzz starts. "Do you want to give us a report, Dick?" "Demo is almost complete," Dick Little states.

"No, it's not. It can't even be 50 percent complete," I reply.

If looks could kill, I'd be gone.

"I watched the placement of the shoring. Very impressive," Dick Little says. Dick the engineer smiles.

"Did anyone see the kitchen slab?" Buzz asks. "No," was said in unison.

"Maybe we better go and look at it. It will hit our budget and potentially our schedule," I say

"No, it won't," Dick Little says.

I roll my eyes.

"Let's just go look at it and go from there," Buzz says, looking at Dick like he's not understanding the program.

The committee walks into the clubhouse and heads into the kitchen. Half of the members were scared to even step on the slab.

One Dick says, "I think I can see where my locker was down below."

"So next steps need to be an assessment and design from Dick the engineer, an H&S estimate, and we'll go from there," Buzz says.

With the building hanging from midair on the shoring and the holes in the kitchen slab, I think everyone was ready to get the hell out of the clubhouse.

As we walk out, I ask Buzz to follow me back to the job-site office. Once we arrive, he sits down in front of my desk.

"Do you want me to wipe off the chair for you?" I ask. "No, it doesn't matter," Buzz says. "I'm already filthy."

"So, the next time we walk through the clubhouse, the committee members must wear hard hats. I'll order some and have them sent here to the job-site office. The other thing is there are plenty of club members wandering around the site, unescorted, without hard hats. If someone gets hurt, I can only imagine the lawsuits at the end of the day. I have a few other ideas. We need to post signs letting the members know the clubhouse is off-limits during construction. Maybe, to curb their enthusiasm about the clubhouse renovation, we can schedule a job-site tour for members once a month. I can conduct the tour, and everyone will have hard hats. Does that sound reasonable?" I ask.

"That sounds great. Why don't you get with D and talk about how to put this plan in place? I like it, Loretta," Buzz states.

Chapter 8

D and I meet a week before the next committee meeting. Buzz gave D the download on my idea, and he's in.

"First, we put signs in the temporary club and on the doors of the clubhouse," I state. "That will be better than we have now, which is nothing."

"When do you want to schedule the walk-through?"

"When are your committee meetings?" D asks. "The last Tuesday of the month at 10 a.m."

"So, we can have them on the last Tuesday at 1 p.m., right after lunch. We can make flyers advertising the tours. I can put a sign-up sheet in the entry of the temporary clubhouse. We need to limit attendance to twenty people, but I doubt we'll get that many. We only have six months to go, so we'll need six tours total," D explains.

"We can print on the flyer to meet at the side entry of the clubhouse, and the tour will take approximately thirty minutes," I say.

D is able to publish the signs and advertisements for next week's tour. The sign-in sheet is sitting next to the front door of the temporary clubhouse. They can't miss it.

I received the spec for the kitchen slab from Dick the engineer last week. I also received thirty hard hats for the job. The kitchen is 2,500 square feet. The spec calls for a reinforcing mesh and a lightweight concrete topping slab. The price from the concrete sub came in just like I expected. High. The total price is $17,000, without H&S's markup. The good news is the time to install the slab will be within the time of the equipment delivery, so there is no schedule delay.

"Hi, everybody. Let's get started," Buzz announces. "Our major issue now is the kitchen slab. Loretta, do you want to take it from here?"

"Sure. Dick the engineer specified a three-inch lightweight concrete with a wire mesh. Our subcontractor quoted $17,000, with no schedule delay. Do you have anything to add, Dick?" I ask.

Dick the engineer says, "I think that is a reasonable price for the amount of work that has to be done."

"So, what does the rest of the committee think about the extra cost?" Buzz asks.

"I think H&S should have anticipated some costs for the floor," Dick Little says. "If they would have anticipated a minor restoration in their original bid, it would not come close to what we have here," Dick Buzzy says.

I smile. "Let's approve the concept. The change order will be submitted by H&S for approval."

"We now want to talk about some rules for the clubhouse. We need to wear hard hats when we go into the construction area. There are hard hats for everyone in the construction job-site office," Buzz says. "So, at the next meeting, we'll have to get hats before we walk around the clubhouse."

"Whose idea was this?" Dick Little asks.

"It was mine," I say. "It has to be followed."

"I disagree. The clubhouse is our private space, and I don't think the members need to wear hard hats walking around our own club," Dick Little announces.

"It is not a private club with private members now. It's a construction site," I say. "Safety protocols have to be followed on all of H&S's construction sites."

"We also have a new rule about the clubhouse. The members are not permitted to enter the clubhouse while it's under construction. We will put signs up notifying all members of that new rule. But to accommodate the interested, we have scheduled a monthly walk for members to join Loretta and walk around the site. Hard hats will be required," Buzz concludes.

"So, does everyone agree that the safety of the club members is important, and we should adopt these rules?" Buzz asks.

All the Dicks nod their heads, except one. Dick Little.

"I agree with the new rule, but I think committee members should be exempt," Dick Little says.

"So, will you sign a release of liability to enter the clubhouse without a hard hat?" Buzz asks.

"Absolutely not!" Dick Little screams.

All the other committee members are sitting there, lips sealed.

"Do the rest of you want to sign a release?" Buzz asks.

"No!" was said in unison. "We'll wear the hard hats."

"So, Dick, we are at an impasse here. You have three choices. Wear the hard hat, sign the release, or be forbidden to enter the clubhouse, which would make it impossible to do your job. Which option would you prefer?"

Chapter 9

I'm sitting at my desk in the job-site office, and the phone rings. "Hi, this is Loretta."

"Hi, this is D. Can you come over to the restaurant?"

"Sure, I'll be right there," I respond.

The restaurant is in the temporary double wides that sit two hundred yards away from the clubhouse.

I walk out of the president's room, head across the drive, and to the parking lot. I see D standing there with a large construction worker. D walks up to me as I approach.

"Hi, Loretta. Thanks for coming over. This guy came into the restaurant, asked to be seated for lunch, and we told him this is a private club and he could not stay here. At that point, he asked to see the manager. That's when I called you," D explains.

"I'll handle it," I announce. I walk up to the construction worker and introduce myself.

"Hi. I'm Loretta. I'm the project manager for H&S on this project. What's your name?"

"My name is Donald."

"Who do you work for?" I ask.

THE COUNTRY CLUB

"I work for Mr. Demolition. This is my first day on the job." "Who is your foreman?" I ask.

"His name is Terry Cantina," Donald says.

"OK, well," I say, "this is a private country club with member-only privileges across the board."

"All I was trying to do was get some lunch here," Donald explains. "And you can't get lunch here. You're not a member," I confirm. "But I'm working here," Donald says.

I hope not for long.

"Let me just ask you, Donald. If you were driving down the highway with your family and saw a sign for the Golden Gate Club-Members Only, would you say, 'Let's get some lunch here'?" I ask.

"No, they would not allow us to eat here because it's a private club."

"Well, Donald," I say, "the same thing applies here."

He looks at me like he's still thinking about our conversation.

"I'm going to find Terry," I say. "Do you know where he is?" I ask.

"No."

"OK, never mind. I'll deal with this on my own."

I go into the men's locker room. Four guys, on a break, are just sitting there.

"Are any of you named Terry?" I ask.

"I'm Terry."

"Well, your new worker, Donald, just tried to eat lunch at the temporary clubhouse," I state. I told him that he is not allowed to eat at the clubhouse. He is not real happy. "I would recommend, maybe, sending Donald back to the union hall and finding another guy."

"And your name is?" Terry asks, with attitude.

"I'm sorry. I should have introduced myself. My name is Loretta. I'm the project manager for the general contractor H&S," I say.

"I'll take care of Donald," Terry says. "Thank you."

I go back to my desk in the job-site office. A member walks in. I look up and see he is upset.

"Hi, can I help you?" I ask. "I'm Loretta."

"Hi. I'm George. I am a member of the club, and I forgot something in my locker. Is there any way I can see if my locker still exists?" he asks. "I left some family pictures in my locker, and I didn't have time to pick them up before the deadline to clean our lockers out," George states.

I look at the time. It's 3:30 p.m. Most of the work is stopped for the day.

"I'll tell you what, George. We can go downstairs and find where your locker was. I can't guarantee anything, but we can go have a look," I explain. "Here, grab a hard hat."

George and I go down the steps and look around. About half of the locker room is demolished.

I turn to George and ask, "Is this where your locker was?"

"Yes. I'll go see if I can find it," George says, smiling.

I let him go alone as I look around at the progress of the demolition.

George comes back in five minutes. "I found them! Thank you so much for bringing me here to get them."

"You are very welcome, George," I say.

As we walk back to the job-site office, George hands me back his hard hat and heads out with his photographs. I sit at my desk smiling, knowing that I took care of someone today.

Chapter 10

I walk into the temporary conference room. Looks like all the Dicks are here.

"Hi, everybody, let's get started," Buzz states.

We don't ask Dick Little for a schedule update anymore. It's a good call not to have him report on anything. H&S has its own daily safety meetings and weekly project meetings. Dick was invited to attend but declined. I'm not sure what he's getting paid for.

Buzz says, "The first tour will be at 1 p.m. today. All the committee is invited." "I'll attend for sure," Dick the architect says.

"I'll join the tour," Dick the engineer says. The kitchen slab is complete, so I'm sure he wants to see that. The demolition of the locker rooms is complete, so I'm sure the members are anxious to see that.

"Dick, are you joining us at 1 p.m.?" I ask Dick Little.

"No, I'm not. I don't agree with these guided tours of the club. The club belongs to the members, and they should be able to do whatever they want to do," Dick announces.

What a spoiled little brat. Do whatever you want to do. Sue the club if you get hurt. Why not? You're a club member.

"Any other business?" Buzz asks.

"Yes," I say. "I want to get the approval of the committee for a barbecue for the construction workers. We can have it on a Monday when the club is closed to members. H&S will sponsor the lunch. Any objections?" I ask.

All members approved the lunch, except one. "I'll move forward with the planning."

At 12:55 p.m., I wait for the others to arrive as I'm standing next to the box of hard hats. A crowd gathers over to the side door, some committee members and D and Buzz.

"Hi, I'm Loretta Novak. I'm the project manager for H&S, the general contractor. I will be your tour guide today. If I could get everyone to get a hard hat and congregate in the hallway."

After everyone has a hard hat, I walk to the front of the crowd in the hallway. "We're going to take a loop around the main floor and then go down to the lower level. You can wander around a little, but stick with the crowd, please. Does anyone have any questions?" I ask.

"Can we keep these hard hats?"

"No, you have to put them back into the box when we get back," I respond. "I heard they are adding a women's locker room. Is that true?"

"Yes. It's small and underneath the front porch, so it will be accessible from the front stairs," I explain.

"What other areas are they going to allow women?"

"I don't know. You'll have to ask Dick or D," I say.

Dick Buzzy jumps in and says, "That kind of information will be issued in the Monthly Club News."

We paraded through the hallway and into the main floor.

"The main living room will get a new wood staircase, new cast stone mantel, new carpet, and wood floor," I say. "The main bar will be brand new from top to bottom, with a coffered wood ceiling. The grand dining room gets enclosed and enlarged, with new carpet and paint."

As we traverse half a flight of stairs, I point to the entrance of the new ladies' locker room and proceed down to the lower level.

"The men's locker room will feature new wood lockers, a spa, a jacuzzi, and will have direct access to the bar and the pool. Beyond that, the grill will be upgraded with carpet and paint."

We exit the club via the new exterior stairs to the driveway. At the top, I say, "Thank you, everyone, for attending. Please put your hard hats in the big box next to the side entrance."

I look at Buzz and D and shrug my shoulders. I get two thumbs up. I smile.

Chapter 11

Contractors get paid for work put in place during the billing month. H&S is having a stellar month at the club. Shoring is installed, excavation is complete, and the kitchen slab is complete. Demolition is 90 percent complete. The pay application submitted for the month of July is $1,250,000. We usually go out of our way at H&S when a client has a large check like this. We usually pick them up in person and immediately take them to corporate accounting. It's sort of a big thing for us.

I get a call from Buzz. "Hi, how are you?" "Fine."

"The check is ready to be picked up," Buzz states.

I look at the clock and see that it's 2:30 p.m. If I leave at 3 p.m., I will be at the downtown club by 3:15 p.m. and have plenty of time to get to the office before they close.

"I'll be there to pick up the check by 3:15," I tell Buzz.

The last thing I would want is the take a million-dollar check home with me.

I drive to The City Club downtown and get a parking space right out front. I walk into the lobby and hit six on the elevator. I'm not sure this is the right floor, but I figure Buzz's office is on the top floor. The elevator doors open, and there are two receptionists there.

I walk in and say, "Is Dick Buzzy available?"

Dick must have heard me because he came running out of his office. "How did you get up here?" Buzz asks

"Well, I walked into the front door, pushed the elevator for floor six, the doors opened, and I walked in, and the elevator proceeded to the sixth floor, the doors opened on the sixth floor, and here I am!"

"You weren't stopped by anyone?" Buzz asks. "No. Should I have been?"

"Yes."

"Do you have the check?" I ask.

Buzz waves an arm as he walks into his office, and I follow. He has a large office, full of club trophies and memorabilia.

"Sit down. Do you want something to drink?" Buzz asks.

"No, I have to get this check to the office before 5 p.m. It's not everyday H&S gets a million-plus check."

I stand up. Buzz hands me the check. I turn and walk toward the elevator lobby.

Buzz says, "Can I ask a favor of you?"

"Sure."

"I need you to walk down the back steps. You really should have been stopped before you came up on the elevator," Buzz states.

"Why?" I ask. "Because I'm a girl?"

Buzz completely ignores my question and comment.

"The back steps lead you to the sidewalk, twenty feet west from the main entrance," Buzz says. "You should be OK. It was good to see you, Loretta."

"Thanks," I smile, sort of.

I walk down the dark stairwell, all six floors of it, and finally open the door to the sidewalk.

I'm blinded by the sunlight when I open the door at the bottom of the stairs. I walk out onto the sidewalk, and my car is parked right there. Perfect. The office is only four blocks away. I start my car and think, *What the hell was that all about? I know it's a private club, but non-members that you are doing business with aren't allowed to use the elevators!*

I pull into the parking garage below the building that H&S's offices are in. "Hi Rich, I'm not going to be long," I say.

"That's what everyone says," Rich giggles.

I walk through the alley, walk into the building lobby, and hit the number fourteen on the elevator buttons. Once I get there, I walk straight to Corporate Accounting to hand them the check. I may have made $500 in interest just by hand-delivering this check.

I drive home, and before I get there, I pull in front of T's house. It's such a nice day. T is sitting outside. I walk up and sit down next to her. She already has a bottle of wine and an empty glass for me on the table.

"So, what's new?" T asks, as she pours me a glass of wine.

"The weirdest thing happened today. I went to the downtown client office to pick up a check for H&S. They seemed stunned I was able to take the elevator to their executive floor without being deterred, without an escort. I was asked to leave via a dark stairwell down six floors to the sidewalk."

"*WHAT?* Do these guys hate women?" T asks.

"No, they're just dicks, and for the last seventy-five years, they didn't have to deal with this women shit, other than at home. Things are changing," I say.

Chapter 12

"Hi, this is Loretta." "Hi, this is Ben." "How are you?" I ask. "Fine, and you?" "Fine."

"I want to know if you can join me for dinner tomorrow?"

Let me think about it.

"Yes," I say.

"Perfect. Bo will pick you up at 2:30 p.m."

"Can he pick me up at the clubhouse?" I ask. "I do have to work tomorrow." "Sure. I have to work as well, so I'll meet you there," Ben says.

Bo makes his way to the Golden Gate Country Clubhouse. He pulls around the circular drive. I'm surprised the limo made it around the curve. I come out of the clubhouse and jump into the car—I mean, limo.

"Where are we going?" I ask.

"You'll find out soon enough," Bo answers.

We arrive at the private jet terminal at SFO. Bo pulls right next to the jet on the tarmac. Ben is standing next to the jet.

I get out of the limo, run toward Ben, and give him a big hug. "What is going on?" I ask excitedly.

"We are going to Spago in LA for dinner," Ben explains.

We both walk onto the small jet and take our seats. Within minutes, the jet pulls back and is cleared for departure. I have never been on a private jet before. It is as nice as everyone thinks. At ten thousand feet, drinks are poured, and we relax.

"Do you have business in LA?" I ask.

"No. Spago owes me a favor, and I just wanted to go to dinner with you," Ben answers.

"What's new?" I ask

"I got a new project in the financial district," Ben shares.

I would have been on that project if I had gotten the job.

"How's Drew?"

"He's doing really good. He's getting married." Ben smiles.

Wow.

We arrive at LAX, and a town car is waiting there for us to get off the plane.

Just like the president and the first lady.

We arrive at Spago thirty minutes later and walk into the restaurant. We are seated immediately. We start with fried calamari, Ben orders an Absolut over with an olive, and I get a bottle of Zinfandel for dinner and a glass for now.

"So, Drew is getting married," I declare as our drinks and appetizers are delivered.

"Yes, he met a gal in Dallas when we were there for a 49er's game. He's head over heels for this gal," Ben says. "When is the wedding?" I ask.

"In September. I'm the best man." Ben smiles. "No way."

As we enjoy our drinks and appetizers, the owner, Wolfgang Puck, walks over to the table.

"Good evening, Ben. It's good to see you. Dinner is on me tonight, and I assume that makes us all square?" Wolfgang explains.

Ben says, "We're good. Let me introduce you to my friend, Loretta Novak." "What a pleasure to meet you," Wolfgang says.

"The pleasure is absolutely all mine." I smile.

"Welcome. My name is Sam, and I'll be your waiter this evening."

I order the grilled lamb, and Ben gets the New York steak. Sam delivers the meal, and it is fabulous as we try to keep the conversation going.

"So, how is the country club project going?" Ben asks.

"It's a project run by a committee, and all the members are named Dick!" I laugh.

"You won't have a problem with that; I know you," Ben concludes.

"Thanks, but there are some arrogant assholes on the committee that aren't really interested in this project. I'm not sure what they are interested in, but it's not managing this project. Remember how focused and interested you were in the 333 Folsom Street project?"

"Well, I had had a lot at risk if we didn't pull it off. But we pulled it off," Ben states and smiles.

"Maybe that's it. There is no risk for the committee members on the job, so why be interested in it?"

As we are finishing our glass of wine, Sam, the waiter, comes up to our table and says, "I apologize for all the commotion," the waiter says.

"What commotion?" Ben asks.

"The man at the table next to you had a heart attack. The paramedics came in and took him to the hospital," the waiter says.

"Oh, we didn't notice. We were talking," Ben states.

"Oh," Sam says.

Chapter 13

The next day, first thing in the morning, which is about 9 a.m. for me, the phone rings in the job-site office.

"Hi, this is Loretta."

"Hi, Loretta. It's Wayne from the pro shop. Do you have a minute to come up here, please?" he asks.

"Sure, I'll be there in about ten minutes," I say. "Thanks."

I find Bill and ask him if he knows anything about the pro shop. "No. Nothing," Bill states.

"I'll be back in a while. I got a call from Wayne. I'm going to meet with him now." "OK," Bill says

I walk past the blooming flowers that they water every day. It's so beautiful here. I venture up to the pro shop, open the front door, and walk in.

"Are you Loretta?" Wayne asks.

"Yes. It's nice to meet you," I say, and I extend my hand to him.

"Well, I have a little issue. One of your workers has been sitting up on the flat here, at 6 a.m., where everybody drives past and is selling golf balls. Do you know anything about this?" Wayne asks.

"No, sir, I don't. Do you know his name?" I ask.

"No," Wayne says. "I never confronted him, but I need to because he is cutting into our profits."

"I understand," I say. "What is it you'd like me to do? Should we plan a sting operation for tomorrow?"

Wayne smiles. "I have been thinking about how to do this, and I decided I need an accomplice. If you try to buy balls from him, I can approach him while you are making the transaction, and it should be fairly calm and straightforward."

I laugh. "I think both of us can just walk over there and tell him what's going on," I suggest.

"That's fine," Wayne agrees.

"Does that mean I have to be here at 6 a.m.?" I ask. *Wayne doesn't know me very well.* "Yes. Tomorrow, I'll meet you at 5:45 a.m., and we both will put an end to this," Wayne declares.

My alarm goes off at 4:45 a.m. I struggle to get dressed, get into the car, and onto the road by 5:15. I pull into the parking at the club, and Pepe is nowhere to be found. I walk up the hill and walk into the pro shop at 5:55 a.m. Wayne is there.

"Do you want a cup of coffee?" he asks.

"Yes, please," I say.

At 6 a.m., Wayne and I walk over to the card table that is set up close to the driveway, with egg cartons filled with golf balls. A sign reads *Dozen balls $10.00*.

"Hi, my name is Loretta from H&S, and this is Wayne from the pro shop at Golden Gate Country Club."

We get a blank stare from the guy sitting at the table. I offer my hand, but he just sits there. Wayne hasn't said a word.

"What's your name? I ask. "Mel."

"Mel, this is Wayne." They shake hands. "He manages the pro shop. Who do you work for?" I ask.

"Hard Drywal."

"Who is your foreman?" "Tony Bertelli," Mel says.

"Well, Mel, you can't sell your golf balls here anymore," I explain.

"But I get them out of a pond in my subdivision. There are thousands of them from the golf course. They must not be very good golfers," Mel states.

"This is the last day you are setting up shop here. Go sell them somewhere else," I suggest.

Wayne and I walk back to the pro shop. Mission accomplished! I start looking around since I've never been in the pro shop before.

"Thanks, Loretta. That worked pretty well. Let me know if you see something that catches your eye." Wayne says. "I have special deals for people like you."

I'm looking around, and suddenly, I see a black hooded light jacket that I just have to have.

"Wayne, I like that black jacket, and I think you have my size." I smile. "It's yours." Wayne smiles back. "Thanks!"

I walk back to the clubhouse and go for a walk around the site. I see the area the drywallers are working in, and I ask, "Is someone here named Tony?"

A very tan, tall man comes forward and says, "I'm Tony. What can I do for you?" "Well, one of your guys, Mel, has been selling golf balls on the way into the club. He has a little table set up with egg cartons full of golf balls." *I can see Tony cracking up a little.* "I think he made a little money, but we shut him down this morning. Maybe you might want to talk to him about it."

I look at Tony, and he has the bluest eyes I've ever seen. "And who are you?" Tony asks.

"Oh, sorry, I should have introduced myself. I'm the project manager for H&S on the project. My name is Loretta."

"Nice to meet you, Loretta." Tony smiles. "Thanks for dealing with Mel this morning. Can I offer you a drink after work today to make up for the issue?"

"Sure, that sounds good."

The most important thing I can do as a project manager is develop a relationship with the subcontractors.

I walk back to the job-site office and sit down at my desk. It's been a long morning so far, but I can't seem to get Tony's blue eyes out of my mind. At 3 p.m., I put on my new hooded jacket from the pro shop. I love it. I told Tony I'd meet him at the Harbor Bar, just north of the country club. I start to walk to my car, and Buzz finds me in his golf cart.

"Hey, want to get together later?" Buzz asks

"I want to, but I can't. I already have a commitment." "OK, the least I can do is give you a ride to your car," Buzz says.

I smile, jump in the cart, and say, "We took care of the guy selling golf balls today."

"I know. I already got the report from Wayne. He was ecstatic," Buzz proclaims.

I smile and jump out of the golf cart. "Thanks. Talk to you soon."

I get in the Miata and drive up the road to the Harbor Bar. I park, get out, walk in, and see Tony sitting at the bar. "Hi," I say.

"Hey, there you are," Tony says.

And there are those blue eyes. I smile.

"Have a seat. What's your pleasure?" Tony asks. It made me flustered as he said that. "I'll have a red zinfandel," I say.

Tony calls the bartender over and orders for me and another for him. I just sit tight. Once the drinks arrive, I ask, "So, how long have you worked for Hard Drywall?"

"I started in the trades when I was eighteen years old and picked Hard after a few years of working for other companies. What about you? How did you get to be a project manager at H&S?" Tony asks.

"I got a civil engineering degree from the University of Pittsburgh," I explain. "Pittsburgh, as in Pennsylvania?" Tony asks.

"Yes, I was recruited out of college to a company in South San Francisco. They recruit outside of California because engineers are more willing to relocate. Californians tend to stay in California. They did international work, and I was interested in a project overseas. Unfortunately, I was transferred to South Carolina, not South America."

"When was this?" Tony asks. "Ten years ago," I say.

"So, I'm going to guess we are about the same age," Tony concludes. "I think we are. I'm thirty-five. How old are you?"

"Thirty-six. Are you married?"

"No."

"Are you married?" I ask.

"Divorced, no kids," Tony reveals.

The inquiry continues.

"Where do you live in the bay area?" I ask

"I rent a place in Marin. It's a nice and short commute to the city and the country club," Tony explains. "Where do you live?"

"I rent in a triplex in East Marin, just over the bridge. Owning a home in the Bay Area was never an option, even at thirty-five and with a good job! I like to know where I am, and the triplex has great views of the city and bridges. It's not an apartment in the suburbs with a view of the pool and the parking lot." Tony laughs, and his blue eyes get brighter as he laughs. "Maybe we can have dinner sometime in Marin. I know a great Italian restaurant in Larkspur," Tony suggests.

"I'd like that," I admit.

The most important thing I can do as a project manager is develop a relationship with the subcontractors.

He smiles, and so do his eyes.

We both pay for our drinks and head to our cars.

"Thanks for the company," I say. "I'll see you at the job site."

Tony waves, smiles, jumps in his truck, and heads down the road.

Well, that was pleasant.

I drive away thinking he must have grown up in a large Italian family with a name like Bertelli. I pull into T's driveway. It's only 6:00 p.m.

"Hi," I say as she opens the door.

"Come on in," T says. "Where were you?"

I sit down in front of the window with the view. T brings a bottle of wine and two glasses.

"I went to happy hour with the drywall foreman, and he has blue eyes to die for," I say.

"WHAT?"

"And last week, I had dinner at Spago's in Los Angeles via a private jet." I smile. "WHAT?"

Chapter 14

It's cold and foggy most days at the clubhouse. By the afternoon, it gets sunny and warm—sixty-five degrees warm, not eighty degrees warm.

Buzz walks into the job-site office. I look up from my desk and smile.

"Hi." Buzz is a tall, thin man, maybe forty, with salt-and-pepper hair, very handsome. "Do you want to want to go golfing with me today?" Buzz asks. "Mondays, the course is closed to members and open to staff. You've been here a few months now, and I thought you'd be ready for a break."

The most important thing you can do as a project manager is develop a relationship with the client.

"Heck yeah," I say. It is perfect golf weather. "Do you have your clubs?" Buzz asks.

"I always have my clubs!"

"Meet me on number one at 11:30," Buzz says. "See you then."

I walk down to my car to retrieve my clubs. As soon as I turn around, my friend, the landscaper, is ready to take me to the first tee. When I arrive, Buzz is already there, warming up with a few swings. He looks at me as I get out of the landscaper's cart and says, "Who is that? A friend of yours?"

"Actually, he gives me a ride to the clubhouse every day."

I grab my clubs out of his cart, put them in our cart, grab a driver, and walk over to the tee box.

"Are you ready?" Buzz asks.

"I don't know, but let's go for it."

The next eighteen holes took it all out of me. I was nervous. This is a hard course, with hills, trees—lots of trees. Buzz is a good golfer, and he was very patient with my game.

"Everyone said you are a good golfer," Buzz explains.

"And you believed them?" I joke. "Sorry to disappoint you, but this course is hard. I haven't played in months, and I usually have a few beers to calm me down during the round."

"Excuses, excuses." Buzz smiles. "Can I take you out for a drink and maybe dinner?" Buzz asks. "It might calm you down."

"Sure," I say. "I do need to go back to the job site and collect some things. If you take me to my car and drop my clubs off, I can drive up to the clubhouse and meet you in fifteen minutes. Is that OK?"

"Perfect!"

I grab my laptop and put it in the trunk of my car. Buzz swings into the circular drive to pick me up. "You can leave your car right there. I'll tell D it's OK," Buzz says.

We head to dinner at an Italian joint out in the avenues. I don't know how to take Buzz. I don't know a lot about him. This might be an opportunity to get to know him. We pull up to Villa Nova on 34th Avenue. Buzz gets out, walks around the car, opens my car door, and holds his hand out for me.

"Thank you," I say.

"You're welcome." Buzz smiles.

We are seated with a carafe of red wine and menus. After welcoming the wine and quickly reviewing the menu, I ask, "So, are you married?"

"No, just divorced," Buzz explains. "I'm sorry. It must be tough." "I'm OK."

"Thanks for inviting me to dinner," I say as I take another sip of wine.

"You're welcome. It isn't every day that a good-looking girl comes to work on the construction project at the club!" Buzz exclaims.

"How long have you worked here?" I ask.

"Six years. Before that, I was managing a golf resort in Arizona," Buzz answers. "Is this the first remodel at the club?" I ask.

"Yes. I'm not looking forward to it. Members with opinions are like assholes.

Everyone has one," Buzz declares.

I laugh.

Dinner is served, and we enjoy every minute of it. I don't think we realized how hungry we were. We walk outside to the car, and Buzz turns to me and gives me a hug.

The Country Club

"Thank you for golfing and dinner today." I smile. "You're welcome."

We drive back to the club, get out of the car, and just stare at each other.

"I do have one more question for you. Why do you call me Buzz?" he asks. "Because I have too many Dicks on this project!"

Buzz smiles and says, "I hope we can do this again. If not the golf, the dinner and drinks."

He probably will never want to golf with me again.

He kisses me very softly, but I pull back just to say, "Thanks. I had a great time."

It's too late to stop at T's for a glass of wine. I guess I'll just go home and get a glass of wine and think about Buzz. I think he actually called me a good-looking girl.

Chapter 15

So, this is the sixth committee meeting and our second tour. We all file into the conference room and take our respective seats. I always sit on the inside, next to the wall. Buzz always sits at the front, and Dick Little always sits to the right of Buzz, like he's his best friend. *Nothing can be further from the truth.*

"So, let's get started," Buzz announces. "Loretta, can you give us a schedule update?"

"My pleasure. We finalized the men's locker order. It's twelve weeks out. The carpet needed to be finalized this week. It will be twelve weeks out as well. Drywall has started. Of course, electrical, plumbing, and HVAC are about 40 percent complete."

I look up at Buzz and nod, indicating I'm done.

"Thanks, Loretta," Buzz says. "Does anyone else have something to bring up?"

"Actually, I do," I say.

"OK, let's hear it," Buzz states.

"Well, H&S has received the change order for the concrete kitchen slab rejected. If my memory serves me correctly, we all sat in this meeting talking about the scope and cost of this work, and H&S was told to proceed. I also remember there is no schedule impact to add this work. So, why has it been rejected?" I ask.

Everyone looks at Dick Little, expecting an answer. Dick Little just looks at me like I'm the one who's got this all wrong. Still not responding, Dick Buzzy says, "So Dick, we need an explanation for rejecting the cost. We are trying to take care of business here, and you don't necessarily want to cooperate."

"I didn't agree that the slab renovation should be an extra cost of work. I mentioned that in our meeting that day," Dick says.

"But none of us agreed with you," Buzz says. "From a committee perspective, the committee approved the work and cost. So, does Dick Little have the authority to reject the cost? The work is done."

"I think it needs to be approved, not rejected," Dick the engineer says.

"HERE, HERE!" says the rest of the committee.

Dick Little tried, but he did not have the authority outside of the committee.

"So, D, do you have some attendees for the tour today?" I ask. "About fifteen. That will work," D says.

"Any feedback from the first tour?" I ask.

"These guys aren't feedback kind of guys unless they have something to gripe about," D explains.

"Are we done?" I ask. "I need to prepare for the tour. If you don't mind, I'll excuse myself. Any of you coming on the tour?"

Silence.

"Just thought I'd ask."

At 1 p.m., the crowd of fifteen gathers at the box of hard hats.

We start the tour through the front door, realizing there are no wall and floor finishes. Walking through the kitchen, it looks ready for equipment; it's just a big empty room.

Equipment is quite a few weeks out. The tour heads for the lower level and walks into the men's locker room. The expression on everyone's face is amazement. It's just one big empty room, as well. Not a lot to talk about.

We peek into the men's spa and shower. It's just getting started. We finish the tour by walking out of the exterior doors leading to the stairs by the new excavation, then walking up the steps that take the tour back to the circular drive.

"Thanks, everyone. Hard hats in the box," I announce.

Chapter 16

The roof on the clubhouse is old-style clay tile. Who knows how old it is? The plans call to remove all the existing tile and intermingle it with new tile to create a blend of old and new tile; dark and light colors of red, yellow, and orange. I assumed they have equipment to remove, raise, and lower the tiles from the roof. The roofing sub asks H&S if they can use the circular drive as a staging area. All the shoring, excavation, and concrete are complete at the end of the drive, so I call D.

"Hi, this is Dick. Can I help you?"

"Hi, this is Loretta. How are you?" I ask. "I'm fine," D says. "What's going on?"

"The roofing sub wants to know if they can use the circular drive as a staging area. According to Diego, their foremen, they should only take one week to complete the work."

"Sure. I'll let the head landscaper know it's OK for the roofers to be there and maybe to water after they are done each day," D says.

"Perfect, D. Thanks."

I give Diego the green light. A few pallets of new clay tile arrive this afternoon. Diego instructs the delivery to be dropped in the middle of the circle, almost right in front of the main entrance. They will start the roof demolition/installation tomorrow. I'm excited to see how they do this.

I get to work a little early, which is odd for me, to see how the roofers get going. I park my car and catch a ride with Pepe up the hill, walk into the job-site office, and make a pot of coffee. Bill never makes coffee in the morning, but he sure drinks it. I pour myself a cup and walk outside to see what the roofers are doing.

To my astonishment, Diego stations himself in front of the pallets of new tiles. Suddenly, I see a tile come flying off the roof. Mateo, who is stationed at the end of the circle, catches the tile and stacks the existing tile toward the back. A section of tile is removed to establish a stockpile of existing tile.

While the demo keeps going, from Santiago on the roof to Mateo in the circle, Juan is ready to start installation. Diego picks up a new tile and throws it up to Juan, who is on the roof, which is at least thirty feet high. At the same time, Santiago is removing the tiles and throwing them down to Mateo. Mateo is throwing an existing tile to Diego, who throws it up to Juan.

It is like a circus, a juggling act. There is always a tile flying through the air, and these guys don't miss a beat. On their break, I ask Diego if they ever use equipment.

Diego says, "We don't need no stinkin' equipment."

The Country Club

I stop at T's on the way home. The weather is great, and the city looks fabulous at this time of day.

"What's new? Been on any private jets lately?" T laughs.

"No, I watched guys throw clay roof tiles around at the country club like it was a circus act. It was pretty amazing, and they didn't even break any. What about you?" I ask.

"I had a twenty-thousand-dollar sale today. My commission is nice on that much money," T applauds herself.

I clap my hands and say, "That's awesome! When are we going to celebrate?" I take a sip of wine T poured for us.

"I don't know. I am pretty happy right now." T smiles.

Chapter 17

The first day of summer is here, and as usual, it is a cold and foggy day. Warm, summer weather only teases you for a few days in Northern California. Then it's back to fog and cold. I'm going through in my head what I'm going to say in the meeting. *The construction is moving along. Demo is complete. The shoring is removed, and the backfill has started. The huge hot tub in the men's locker room is being built.* I walk over to the temporary clubhouse and walk into the conference room. I see Buzz and D. They both smile at me. I walk over to him, and I sit down next to him. It's 9:45 a.m., but no one else is here.

"Hi, where is everybody?" I ask.

"I don't know," Buzz says. "Maybe everyone is on vacation and won't be joining us today."

"Did anyone text you or something to notify you that they would not be here today?" I ask.

"No, I heard nothing," Buzz admits.

These guys are just stellar.

The Country Club

At 10 a.m., there are still no committee members in the room. Buzz looks at me and asks, "Do you want to go to lunch somewhere?"

I say, "Sure. If this meeting isn't going to happen, we may as well go to lunch. Oh, the tour is at 1 p.m. today, so we'll have to be back by then."

D says, "No one signed up for the tour today either."

"Really?" I ask. "I'm not going on a tour by myself. Sounds like lunch is on."

Buzz and I walk out of the conference room. "Bye, D," I say. We walk over to the job-site office, walk in, and see Dick Little chatting with Bill.

"You missed the committee meeting," Buzz says.

"Bill and I were talking about fishing, and I must have lost track of time," Dick explains.

"Well, we canceled the meeting because no one else showed up either," Buzz says. I grab my purse. Buzz and I start to walk out of the office.

"Where are you two going?" Bill asks.

"I'm taking Loretta to lunch," Buzz says.

"Can we go with you?" Bill and Dick Little say in unison.

"No. Sorry. We'll be back later," Buzz says as we walk out of the office. His car is parked in the circular drive, so we jump in and drive to the highway.

"How about we go south to Half Moon Bay and not north into The City?" Buzz says.

"That's fine with me. I haven't been to Half Moon Bay in at least ten years."

"We can go to Sam's Chowder House. It's maybe only thirty minutes from here," Buzz says.

"Sounds good to me, and the drive sounds nice too," I say.

We turn left out of the club and go south along the coast. The view of the ocean is spectacular. We make our way to Highway 1 and Pacifica. Highway 1 continues past Montera Beach to Half Moon Bay. We finally stop at Sam's. It is a clear day at the beach. No fog, very little wind, and a temperature in the low seventies. I open my car door, and Buzz walks over and grabs my hand. I stand up from the car, and I am just about blushing in front of him. He puts his arms around me and gives me a big hug and finishes with a kiss. I smile.

"Thanks for bringing me here," I say.

"The pleasure is all mine."

Buzz smiles as we walk toward the restaurant. There is a large patio with seating overlooking the pacific. It's fabulous. We get a table for two on the patio. We sit down and enjoy the view for a moment. The sound of the ocean just about drowns out the voices of the patrons.

A waitress comes by our table, hands us menus, two glasses of water, and says, "Can I get you something to drink?"

"I would like a vodka tomato juice, a splash of Worcester, and a dash of celery salt," I say

"I'll take a gin and tonic," Buzz says.

"I'll be right back with your drinks." "What is your name?" I ask

"Dusty," she says, turning to get our drinks.

The Pacific Ocean is loud and fierce when the waves crash into the rocks. We start to look at the menu.

"I already know what I'm getting. What looks good to you, Buzz?" I ask.

"Oysters on the half shell," Buzz says.

"That's the same thing that I was going to order. Why don't we get at least a dozen and some garlic bread?" I smile.

Dusty walks over with our drinks and asks if we are ready to order.

Buzz states, "We'll have a dozen oysters on the half shell and a loaf of garlic bread." Dusty says thanks and walks away with our order.

"I didn't know you liked oysters," Buzz says.

"I love them, and I don't know why. They are slimy little things, but they taste great.

But I do have to admit, I like the little wee ones, not the big ones."

I stare at Buzz, and he smiles. Today's lunch was an unexpected pleasure.

Chapter 18

It's July and time for golf. I get the invitation and respond with a foursome at the annual Lake Tahoe golf tournament. I invited Ben, Carroll, and Drew to play with me. Ben is picking up the hotel rooms for everyone.

On Friday, at 11 a.m., Ben comes to pick me up at the cabin, Ben's new nickname for my triplex. I pack my suitcase and my golf clubs into the Jeep. *I guess he left the limo at home.* The two of us head up the hill to Lake Tahoe, one of the most beautiful places on Earth.

When we arrive in South Lake Tahoe, we pull up to the valet, and the bellboys surround the car, open the doors for us, and take the luggage out of the trunk. We leave the golf clubs in the car for tomorrow. We check into a suite with two bedrooms, a deck, and a view of the lake. Absolutely stunning. The cocktail party starts at 5 p.m., with heavy appetizers and the lineup for tomorrow.

Ben and I walk onto the patio at the clubhouse. I see that Carrol and Drew have a table, so we head in that direction. I get a hug from Carroll and Drew. I look at the crowd as I hug Drew and see Lee and Jen, and it looks like they are walking our way.

Once they get to the table, I say, "Hi, Lee," and give him a big hug.

"Hi, Jen," I say, and give her a hug too. We only see each other once a year—here. "So let me introduce you. Lee, Jen, this is Ben Swimmer, Carroll Hanson, and Drew Henderson. I had the pleasure of working with these guys on the 333 Folsom project last year."

Lee walks over to Ben and shakes his hand. "Nice to meet you. Welcome to our tournament." Lee shakes hands with Carroll and Drew. "Welcome, get a drink and some food. I hope you enjoy playing golf tomorrow." Lee is a fantastic host. Meanwhile, I was able to chat with Jen.

We say bye to Lee and Jen and order drinks from the waiter, and then the guys go to the food bar. I look around and don't recognize many people. It doesn't matter. I'm here with my favorite guys. It's going to be a great weekend.

At 7 p.m., we go to the top floor of the casino; the restaurant is on the top floor. The line for dinner winds all the way back to the elevator lobby.

Ben announces, "Wait here. I'll be right back." In less than three minutes, Ben is back with a waiter, who shows us to our table. I look at Ben, shrug my shoulders and hands, palms up, thinking, *How did that happen?*

He looks at me, smiles, and says, "VIP."

We get seated. I'm just glad Carroll hasn't started in on me about Ben. Maybe he is classy enough not to go there in front of Ben and Drew.

"So, Loretta, what are you working on these days?" Carroll asks.

"I'm on the Golden Gate Clubhouse renovation project. It's management by committee, so that's been challenging. Plus, they are all named Dick." Everyone starts laughing.

Dinner is finally served, and it is delicious. During the meal, the sunset and lake were the perfect backdrop.

The next day, our foursome tees off at 10:40 a.m., so we were able to have breakfast and get to the course to practice—like that's going to help—by 9:30 a.m. Lee drives his cart over to say hi to everyone because he's teeing off right now. "See you in the clubhouse. Have a great round." He waves as he drives to the first tee.

We are organizing everything that we need during the round—golf balls, tees, golf gloves—and positioning them all in our golf cart. Ben looks in my golf bag and says, "You need new headcovers."

"No, these are fine," I say.

"If you did get some new ones, what kind of animals would you want?" Ben asks. "Hmmm. I have to think about that. How about a monkey and a cow?" I say. "Why?" Ben asks.

"Why not?"

After a five-hour round, we all shake hands on the eighteenth green. I don't think any one of us had that good of a round, but as a team, we did great with our handicap. Drew wrote his name down for closest to the pin on number twelve, and I wrote my name down for the ladies' longest drive on number sixteen. It doesn't mean we'll win because there are a lot of golfers behind us, still playing. But we'll find out soon enough.

We turn our scorecard in and head to the bar. By the time everyone had finished, it was close to 5:00 p.m. They had the scores tallied and the winners' names on the money envelopes.

Lee stands front and center at the patio bar and whistles. Everyone pipes down. "Thanks for coming..." He reads the closest-to-the-pin winners first. "And on number twelve, at four foot nine, Drew Henderson!" We all scream and clap for him. "And for the ladies' longest drive, Dana Parks!"

"Dammit, I never win." Drew sits back down and opens his envelope. He just won a hundred bucks!

"You're buying the next round!" Ben screams.

Next is the winning foursomes. Lee starts with, "And in third place..." and then, "In second place, with 121, Loretta Novak, Drew Henderson, Ben Swimmer, and Carroll Hanson."

Everyone cheers and whistles. All four of us walk up to accept our prize and get our picture taken with Lee.

They score differently at this tournament. Each player records their handicapped score. Then, the team records three scores on par threes, two scores on par fours, and one score on par fives. So, our score, 121, is 15 under par!

Back at our table, we cheer to our success. Lee walks over and says, "I've played in this tournament for fifteen years and have never won a thing! What are your plans for the evening?" Ben says. "We have reservations at the dinner show venue with Chris Isaac. Would you like to join us?"

Lee didn't hesitate to say, "Sure, we'd love to join you."

"When you get there, just show them your ID, and you'll be on the list," Ben explains. Lee likes important people, and Ben qualifies.

So, after a shower, a shave, and another drink, we head to the hotel ballroom. We get escorted into the room and seated in the front row booth. *Must be a VIP thing again.* Lee and Jen are already seated, with large smiles plastered on their faces. We order drinks just when Carroll and Drew arrive. Even Drew says, "Wow. This is close."

The meal was fabulous, and we were all excited to see Chris Isaac. Even Carroll was all smiles.

At breakfast the next day, we again eat VIP-style at the penthouse buffet.

Carroll and Drew are sitting down by the time Ben and I get to the table. "I see you don't have any eggs," Carroll says.

"I'm allergic to eggs," I say. "So, Drew, Congratulations. I hear you're getting married," I say.

"Yes, I'm very happy and excited."

"Where is the wedding?" I ask.

"I grew up in Monterey, so we picked a beach venue for the wedding there."

"We better get going. I have an employee barbecue tomorrow at the project. I don't want to get home too late."

We all stand and hug each other. What a great weekend!

Chapter 19

Today is the big barbecue. The club generously let us use some tables and chairs. They even helped us set up the circular drive for the event. The event is a construction worker celebration that Bill was able to sponsor with the money he received from selling the marble toilet partitions. It's Monday, and the golf club is closed to the members. H&S has the place to ourselves.

Meathead BBQ is working the event, and I have an area for them to set up, cook, and serve in the circle. At 10:30 a.m., Meathead BBQ shows up with the grub. It takes them one hour to set out the food, utensils, and beverages. At 11:30 sharp, the workers start to file in line for the tri-tip, fried chicken, corn on the cob, mashed potatoes, and cornbread. I stand back to make sure everything is OK and see Buzz walking over.

"Can I sit with you?" Buzz asks.

"Sure, I'd love that." I smile as we move to our place in line for the food.

Buzz and I make our way through the food line and find seats.

"These guys must love this," Buzz says.

"I'm sure they do."

"I got a call from Dick Little this morning, saying he didn't think this BBQ was appropriate. He questioned who was paying for it," Buzz stated.

"That doesn't surprise me. H&S—or should I say Bill—sold demoed material for $750, and we are using it today to pay for the barbecue. I'm sure Dick will object to that too. He objects to everything," I complain.

We see the other Dicks in the food line. That's great. Buzz and I walk over to say hi.

"This is great, Loretta," Dick the engineer says. "I agree. These guys deserve a break," Dick says. Buzz and I walk back to the job-site office.

"This was a great event. I'm impressed." Buzz smiles. "Do you want the phone number for Meathead BBQ?" "Sure," Buzz says. "Are you free for dinner tonight?"

"I am," I smile. "Maybe a light dinner after that barbecue lunch."

"Great. You can leave your car in the circle like you did last time. I'll let D know, and we can hit happy hour at around 4 p.m." Buzz explains.

"That's perfect. I have to supervise Meathead BBQ cleanup and exit, and that will give me plenty of time to catch up on what is going on with construction today. I'm thinking not a whole lot."

Buzz stops to pick me up at 4 p.m., and we head to The City but stay on the beach and pull into a small diner right on the cliff of the ocean. I look up and smile as I get out of the car. He walks over to where

THE COUNTRY CLUB

I'm standing to hold my hand. It is very windy, and we are close to the cliffs. The views are great. We walk in, and the waiter approaches.

"Hi, Mr. Buzzy. Nice to see you again. We have a fabulous corner window-view table for you."

We both follow him to the table. I sit down and cannot believe the view of the ocean. There is no fog, and the wind seems to be picking up the waves perfectly.

We look at the menus, and I ask, "What are you going to have? What's good here?"

"I do come here often, and the food is great. My favorite is the fish and chips, but it's a big dish. We can split it, and that would be perfect."

The waitress comes over to the table. "Hi, Buzz. Do you want the usual?" "Yeah, but Jane, I want to introduce you to my friend, Loretta."

"Hi." I smile.

"We have shrimp louie for our special. What can I get you to drink?" Jane asks. "I'll have a gin and tonic," I answer.

"I'll be right back with your drinks," Jane says. "Do you like deep-fried calamari?" Buzz asks.

"Yes. And I'd be fine with just that after our big barbecue," I explain. "A gin and tonic is a change for you," Buzz states.

"This place reminds me of porch-sitting in Pittsburgh. On summer nights, one of my friends was renting an ex-fraternity house that had a huge front porch. And, for whatever reason, we all drank gin and tonics. I think it's a Pittsburgh thing. The view is nicer, but the feel is the same. Plus, I have a doctor's appointment in The City tomorrow," I disclose.

Jane delivers the calamari, and we order another round of drinks. "Is anything wrong?" Buzz questions with concern.

"No, I had two outpatient procedures related to my cervix with negative results, but my doc wants a second opinion. He says it's not cancer, and I believe him," I explain. "I've had a few scares with cancer myself. Melanoma. Probably from my years in Arizona, but I'm good now."

"They say it never goes away completely," Buzz admits.

We squeeze lemon over the entire dish and start nibbling on the calamari. They have fantastic sourdough bread, as well. Our drinks arrive, and Buzz raises his glass and says, "Cheers. It's been a good day."

"Cheers," I echo as we clink our glasses together and smile. "It's just what I needed after today's barbecue," I reveal.

"I really like you, Loretta. I like spending time with you," Buzz says with a sparkle in his eyes.

My heart sinks, and I feel a little dizzy, but I'm at a loss for words.

I'm never at a loss for words.

I smile and hope to come up with something soon. I stare into his green eyes and say, "I'm very attracted to you, too. We do have a few months to complete this project. I don't want this project to come between us."

"Neither do I. Let's take it slow. You have a lot going on." Buzz smiles.

Chapter 20

The next morning, I drive into the avenues instead of the country club. I pull into the parking lot at the doctor's office, get out of the car, and I walk to the building. I hit the elevator call button. The elevator opens, lets me in, and I push the button for the third floor. The elevator opens on the third floor, and I exit into the hallway. My appointment is at 9 a.m., and it is 8:55 a.m. I walk into the office. It looks like it hasn't been remodeled since the fifties. The waiting room is packed. I find a seat and wait for forty minutes until they call my name.

"Loretta Novak? The doctor will see you now."

I follow the receptionist to the back office and am led into the third office on the left.

I walk into the office.

"Good morning. I'm Dr. Shishir Bain. Please take a seat."

I sit down and look around, not really knowing what to think.

"Dr. Adams is a colleague of mine and asked if I could review your chart, which I did. I see you have had two colposcopy procedures with negative results."

"Yes, Dr. Adams said I didn't have cancer."

"I understand that, but my recommendation for you is a full hysterectomy." "*WHAT?*" *I sound like T.*

"A hysterectomy will solve a lot of your future problems," the doctor explains.

"But I don't have any other problems, and I don't have cancer."

"A hysterectomy removes non-vital organs from females. You don't need them to live," Dr. Bain says.

"What if I want to have children?" I ask.

"You are almost past childbearing years, aren't you?" Dr. Bain asks.

"No, I'm not!" I cry. At this point, I stand up, tears in my eyes, and start to walk out of the office.

The doctor says, "We are not done."

"Yes, we are!"

I walk out of the doctor's office and don't know what to do. I'm so pissed off that a well-known doctor in San Francisco can just recommend a hysterectomy because it removes parts that women don't need. I don't have cancer, and I don't have any pain or problems, but according to Dr. Dipshit, it solves all my problems, now and in the future. Fuck him. I'm never going to the doctor again.

It's 2 p.m., and I decide not to go to the country club and go straight home. T must have a bottle of wine at the house, and we can try to sort through what this doctor said over a bottle of wine.

When I get home, I call T. She answers and says she's on her way home too. "Come to my house for happy hour today," I say.

"OK. Are you OK?" T asks.

"Well, we'll talk about it when you get here."

T pulls into the driveway, walks up the steps, and rings the doorbell. I open the door and smile. T walks in. I'm happy to see her.

"It looks like you've been crying. Are you OK?" T asks.

"Some people throw things, swear, and yell when they are angry. I just cry when I am really angry, and I'm really angry."

I get T a glass of wine, refill mine, and we both sit down in front of the view. "The doctor that I met with today wants me to get a hysterectomy," I explain. "He said, 'A hysterectomy will solve a lot of your future problems. A hysterectomy removes non-vital organs from females. You don't need them to live. You are almost past childbearing years, aren't you?'"

"WHAT?" T screams.

"I sat here all afternoon trying to make some sense of it, but the only thing I can think of is this is such a male approach to this issue. I can just imagine if males had some non-vital organs that could conveniently be removed to make all their problems 'go away.'"

"I don't understand how a doctor can be so nonchalant about his 'second' opinion, like it doesn't affect my life at all. He assumes I don't want children, and that is so not right. I'm never going to the doctor again."

"You can't just say you're never going to the doctor again," T explains.

"Yes, I can. It's horrible. I don't know if it's a competence thing like doctors assume I don't know any better because I'm female, and they'll just try this on me. Or maybe it's a male thing, and they do it because they can. But what he said to me was so not right. Have you ever seen the movie *The Stepford Wives*?"

T says, "Yes, that was a scary movie. My life changed a bit after I saw it."

"Mine too. And the saying 'because we can' stuck with me. In so many situations, I think of that and wonder if it is happening 'because they can.' I thought of that today, listening to that doctor. Is he telling me he can remove all my non-vital parts just because he can?"

"You're giving me chills!" T screams.

Chapter 21

"Well, let's get started. Do you want to start with the schedule, Loretta?" Buzz says. "Sure, the carpet and the kitchen equipment have been ordered. They each have a ten-week lead time. Drywall has started. Plumbing, HVAC, and electrical is going full steam ahead. Today, I'm going on a field trip to a hotel in downtown San Francisco that has a stenciled bar—just to see what it looks like."

"What is the CMP schedule showing as the completion date?" Buzz asks. "November 22nd is the current completion date," I state.

"As I stated before, that's not acceptable," Dick Little says.

"Well, we are going to come up with a plan to make the original contract schedule work," I say.

"Which is?" Dick Little asks, with attitude.

He is such a dick.

I want the committee and H&S to agree to a plan. "I think the committee should authorize OT for certain trades each week. Each week, I'll have Bill and the foreman of each trade come up with what trade needs OT. This way is more economical than paying everyone overtime whether or not it's needed."

"We can have Dick Little on point for that each week. OK, Dick?" Buzz asks.

Dick Little gives no acknowledgment. No nodding his head, no changed facial expression, no words.

"Dick? Are you OK with this approach?" Buzz asks again.

He's probably worried he might have to work or something

"This is the only way we will make the original completion date," I say. "Do you agree with that approach?" Buzz asks.

Dick finally says, "Yes, I don't seem to have a choice."

"We can review the amount and cost of overtime in the committee meetings. The fourth tour is today. Does anyone have anything to say about the tours?" I ask.

"Everyone loves them," says Dick.

It's about 3 p.m., and I have been tasked by Dick, the architect, to visit a bar in the Palace Hotel in San Francisco that has similar stenciled beams. It's called Meyers Pub. Sounds like a tough assignment to me. I call Ben.

"Hi, this is Ben." "Hi, this is Loretta."

"Hi, Tiger, how are you?"

"I'm fine. Hey, I have to go to the bar in the Palace Hotel to look at their stenciled beams, and I want to know if you want to join me?" I ask.

"Today?"

"Yes."

"OK, I'm in. I just have a few things to clean up around here. I can meet you there at 4:30 p.m.," Ben explains.

"That's perfect. I'm all the way out at the clubhouse so that works for me. You know the bar, Meyers Pub?" I ask.

"Yes, I like that bar," Ben reveals. "See you then."

I walk to get my car, and Buzz stops and says, "Hey, pretty lady, can I give you a ride?"

"Absolutely."

He pulls up to my car and says, "Are you busy tonight? Can I buy you dinner?" "I'm working. It's tough duty. I have to go to a bar in the Palace Hotel with stenciled beams like those specified for our project." "Do you want me to come with you?" Buzz asks.

"I'd love that, but I already have a friend meeting me there," I say. "Male or female?" Buzz asks.

"Male."

"OK. Let's set something up for next week," Buzz says. "Sounds good."

He waves as he pulls away in his golf cart.

I jump into the Miata and head to the Palace Hotel. I pull up to valet park. I am greeted by an attendant and explain I am going to the Meyers Pub. He smiles and gives me a ticket for my car. I walk down this long hallway and see the door to the bar on the left. I walk in and realize I have been here before. I look around and don't see Ben, so I take a seat at the bar. The bartender approaches and asks if I'd like a drink.

"Yes, a glass of zinfandel, if you have it."

"Would you like to see a wine list?" the bartender asks. "Yes, please."

He gives me a wine list, and I select a Dry Creek zinfandel. He takes my order, and I look up at the stencils on the beams above. It looks beautiful and gives the place a warm, cozy feel. As soon as the bartender serves my wine, Ben walks in.

"Hi, Tiger," he says as he kisses me on the cheek. "I haven't been here in years. It hasn't changed much. I like this place."

Ben orders an Absolut over with an olive, and I stare at the beams on the ceiling. This is what I'm supposed to be doing.

"Tiger, what are you doing?"

"Oh, sorry. I'm just looking at the stenciled beams. It is why I'm here, remember, my field trip to the bar?" I like these kinds of field trips.

Ben's drink is served, and I ask, "So, how was Drew's wedding?"

"It was fabulous. Monterey is a great place for a wedding. I did OK as the best man."

"What does OK mean?" I ask.

"I thought we should do body shots at the reception but had no interest, so we just did tequila shots, no body," Ben explains.

"And the honeymoon?" I ask.

"They went to Hawaii for a week. That's all the time off I gave him," Ben claims. I smile, thinking if I was working for Ben, I'd get one week's vacation.

"How's the clubhouse project going?" Ben asks.

The Country Club

"Well, we are in overtime mode to try and meet the original completion dates after starting two weeks late. The construction manager, Dick Little, says we will have no delays on the project, and we absolutely must be finished by November 8th."

"That's really his name?" Ben asks.

"It couldn't be more appropriate." I smile.

"Tiger, you better get all this in writing because I know guys like this, and they do not have the most integrity in the world," Ben admits.

"I am documenting everything, but I don't know what else to do," I explain.

"So, did you bring a camera to take pictures of the ceiling and prove you were here?" Ben asks.

"Yes, I'll take a few shots on our way out. How is your new project going?" I ask. "Not good. Permits have delayed the start, and the contractor refuses to start without them." *Sound familiar.* "It makes owners and contractors in conflict on the job day one."

"What are you doing for your birthday?" I ask.

"How do you know when my birthday is?" Ben questions.

"Drew told me. I think we can go out and celebrate the big day," I say.

Ben smiles. "That sounds good. I can invite Drew and Carroll if you'd like." "You can invite anyone you'd like," I say.

"It's your birthday; you make the call."

I pay the bill since it is my field trip. We stand up, and I flash a few photos before anyone gets suspicious. It is a nice place.

We walk down the long hallway to the entry to retrieve the cars from the valet.

"Thanks for joining me. I enjoyed seeing you," I say.

"Me too." Ben smiles.

Chapter 22

The committee meeting is about to start. As usual, all the Dicks are in attendance.

Dick Buzzy stands and says, "Welcome. I hope everyone enjoyed the barbecue sponsored by H&S."

"I don't agree with H&S sponsoring this event," Dick Little states. "If there was money received from selling something out of this clubhouse, it should be ours to use, not theirs."

"Would you rather we say you sponsored the lunch?" I ask with attitude.

"I would rather have no lunch at all and pocketed the money," Dick Little admits. "Christ, Dick. The workers deserve a lunch honoring them and their hard work, and this is one way to do it. It helps productivity on the job," Dick Buzzy says. "I still don't agree," Dick Little says.

"Well, it's a done deal. The committee agreed to have the event, and so did the staff at the club. Plus, it was only $700.00," I announce.

Dick Buzzy pipes up and says, "OK. I think we've had enough of this conversation. Let's move on to the overtime costs. Loretta, where are we on total OT costs to date?"

"So far, we have authorized seven drywallers, four hours overtime, each day last week, at the rate of forty bucks an hour. That equals $9,800. If we assume $10,000 of overtime costs for the next ten weeks—August, September to mid-October—that's $100,000, give or take a few man-hours," I explain.

"No way!" Dick Little screams.

"What exactly were you expecting?" I ask.

"A hell of a lot less than that," Dick Little says.

"Well, our other option, and we still have time to do this, is to delete items of work that total $90,000." We already spent $10,000. "Like the stenciled beams, the wood coffered ceiling, things like that," I explain.

"Absolutely not," Dick the architect says. "The items mentioned are the like icing on this cake. It would look unfinished without them."

"I don't know what else we can do but continue overtime, being very careful of what trades to pull in so we can make up enough time to meet the original date. There still are no guarantees. Other things can go wrong," I state.

"What do you mean there are no guarantees? You have a contract that says the project will be complete by November 8th," Dick Little replies.

"I also have a contract that says I will start February 1st. That did not happen. We were two weeks behind schedule on day one. Is this how you do business? The terms of the contract that work for you, work for you, and the terms of the contract that don't work for you, don't apply?" I say.

"That's enough," Dick Buzzy says. "We need to decide what to do, to give H&S some direction. So, what is it, overtime or deletion of finishes? This committee manages this project, so we need a decision. All for continuing with the overtime?" Dick Stone, Leggett, Buzzy, and Blue raised their hands. "All for deleting finishes?" Dick Molinari was the sole backer of deleting finishes. Dick Little didn't make a choice. He's such a terrible leader and manager. I don't know why the club hired him.

"So, let's move forward with the weekly assessment of overtime, and we will summarize where we are at each meeting," Dick Buzzy finalizes.

"We will have a tour at 1 p.m. today if any of you are interested in seeing the progress we are making," I say. "Meet at the usual spot to pick up a hard hat."

Chapter 23

It's Sunday afternoon, all my chores are done, and the sun is shining on the bay. I call T and ask if she wants to go to the yacht club.

"Hell yeah!" T says.

We meet there in thirty minutes. I take my favorite seat at the bar. I smile when T walks in the door.

"What do you want to drink?" I ask. I wave Charles over. "And how are Lolly and Trisha today?" Charles asks. "Fine, and you?" T replies. "I'll take a Myers and O.J." "And you?"

"Yes, please," I say.

Charles knows that when I say "yes, please," it means the usual, which means a glass of red zinfandel.

He returns shortly with our drinks.

"Can we run a tab?" I ask.

"Sure. Enjoy." Charles smiles. "So, what's up?" T asks.

"All kinds of stuff!" "Like what?"

"I told you I went to LA for dinner on a private jet."

"And this was *after* you told him you didn't want to have an affair with him?" T asks. "This is crazy stuff."

"Yes, it is," I say as I take a sip of wine. "How is your dad?"

"He's back at work, and I'm back on the street selling for Spacely Sprocket," T says. "That's good," I say.

I ask Charles for another round. I look up and see Ben Swimmer standing in the yacht club.

"Ben, what are you doing here?" I ask. "This is a private club."

"Actually, I was looking for you," Ben says.

My heart drops. T and Charles were looking at me with confused faces.

"Why?" I ask.

"Because I wanted to hang out with you today," Ben says.

"You could have called." *Enough said.* "Come take a seat, and I can introduce you to my friend and neighbor, Trisha."

"Hi, Trisha. I'm Ben." "Hi," T says.

"And you know Charles, the bartender. Can I get you a cocktail?" I ask.

"Actually, I've been here before, but I've never been formally introduced to Charles," Ben explains.

I wave to Charles, and he makes his way to our end of the bar. "Charles, this is Ben Swimmer."

Ben reaches over the bar and shakes his hand. "Hi, Charles. I'm Ben. Nice to meet you.

I'll take an Absolut on the rocks with an olive."

"Hi, Ben. Lolly has told me a lot about you." Charles smiles.

I look a Charles, with a smile on his face, like what the hell. "Who's Lolly?" Ben asks.

"That's my nickname," I say.

"Oh, sorry. I have my own nickname for you," Ben states.

T is sitting there and has not said a word. She is probably thinking about what Ben's nickname is for me.

Charles delivers Ben's drink, and I get another wine. "So, the 49ers are on at 4 p.m.," Ben states.

"Well, there are no TVs in here," I explain.

"I guess we will have to go to your house to watch the game," Ben says. "T, are you in or not?" I ask.

"You guys go. I'll catch up with you this week," T says. "It was nice meeting you, Ben." She walks out of the club.

"Do you have Absolut and wine?" Ben asks.

"That's a good question. Let's get there first and address the situation."

We wave to Charles, jump in our vehicles, and drive up the hill to the triplex. I pull into the garage, and Ben pulls into the driveway. Together, we make our way up the front steps. I unlock and open the door.

"Welcome."

Ben walks into the house and takes a wide-eyed look at the view.

"So, this is what Drew was so excited about? I can see why. This is spectacular!" Ben smiles.

We get settled and take inventory of the alcohol. I have wine but no vodka. While I was hunting through the kitchen cupboards, Ben went straight for the TV.

"How long have you had this thing?" Ben asks. "Since college."

"I think you need a new one," Ben says.

"The one I have is fine."

I'm not the type that has to have the latest and greatest of anything. When things break or die, I'll get a new one.

"No, it's not. The box is almost as deep as it is wide. Let's go to Costco and buy a new one."

"Now?" I ask.

"Sure, why not? And we can pick up some olives and Absolut while we're there."

"We're probably going to miss part of the game," I mention.

"It's OK."

Chapter 24

Tony walks into the job-site office after the weekly meeting. I look up and smile. He walks over to my desk and says, "I've never been at job central before." His blue eyes mesmerize me.

"Hi, what brings you to job central today?" I ask.

"We are done with our overtime work. They are moving into painting and woodworking, so I'm not working until 7 p.m. anymore, and I want to take you to dinner."

I smile again.

"Is today OK?" Tony asks. "We can meet there on the way home from work." "Sounds good to me. I just need to figure out where to go."

"We're going to Bertelli's in Larkspur," Tony explains. "Isn't that your last name?" I ask.

"We'll have all evening to talk about that," Tony says. "I can follow you from here," I say.

"That's perfect. We can leave at 4 p.m."

"I'll get my car from the contractors' parking lot below and park my car up here in the circle and wait for you. I drive a convertible."

The Country Club

Tony smiles and walks out of the office. I work at my desk, but I'm distracted by those blue eyes. At about 3:30 p.m., I pack up and start walking down to my car. Who do you think pulls up beside me but Buzz?

"Can I give you a ride?" Buzz asks.

"Sure," I say and jump in his golf cart.

We get to my car, and Buzz asks, "Can I buy you a drink tonight?"

"Your timing sucks. I already have plans. We need to schedule something next week."

He smiles, shaking his head, as I climb out of his golf cart. I smile and wave. I drive the Miata to the circle, park, and go into the office. I grab my computer and lock up the office. As soon as I walk back to the car, Tony pulls up in his truck, winds down the window, and says, "Are you ready?"

I smile, nod, and get in my car. He leads off, and we pull out of the circle drive and out of the country club. The drive from Highway 35, the great highway along the beach, is beautiful. We meander through city streets and the Presidio to the Golden Gate Bridge. This is my commute every day.

I am still following Tony across the bridge, onto the freeway to the Larkspur exit. We make our way to Bertelli's, and I follow Tony's truck into the parking lot. He gets out of his truck and approaches my car. I open the door, and he lends a hand. I can smell Italian food from here. I grab hold of his hand, and he helps me stand up. We walk through the parking lot and into the restaurant.

"Hello, Antonio. It's good to see you."

They hug and backslap each other. I just stand and watch.

"Loretta, this is my brother Angelo," Tony says.

"Hi, Angelo." I hold my hand out and shake his hand. "I'm Loretta. Nice to meet you," I say.

We are seated at Tony's favorite table. At this point, I'm really interested in the story about this place. Angelo distributes the menus—not like Tony needs a menu.

"Your brother calls you Antonio?"

"Yes, my whole family does."

"So, does your family own this place?" I ask.

"Yes. I own a quarter of it," Tony says.

Angelo takes our drink order, which is a bottle of red zinfandel, while I look at the menu.

"So, what's your favorite thing on the menu?" I ask. "Pork Milanese," Tony says.

"Mine is spaghetti and meatballs."

Angelo uncorks the bottle of wine and pours a glass for each of us.

"Tell me about growing up in this family," I say.

"OK. My grandfather started a sausage company that grew into wholesale and retail stores. My sister and brothers all went to work for the company, but I went to work in the trades. I didn't want to work for the family company."

"But you got a piece of the restaurant."

"Yes, I was offered the deal, and I took it," Tony explains.

Angelo starts us off with fried calamari and sourdough bread. He refills our wine glasses while he is at the table.

"Am I supposed to order?" I ask.

"No, we have a medley of dishes coming for you to taste," Tony says. "OK," I say as I take a sip of wine.

The next round was mozzarella on flatbread.

"Oh my, this is my favorite so far," I say. "Did you ever work here?"

"When I was a teenager, I worked as a busboy. I knew then that this was not the business for me."

Angelo arrives with a small plate of spaghetti and one meatball.

"What are you ordering?" I ask.

"Pork Milanese, my favorite," Tony says.

I try the meatball, and my eyes roll around. It is so good. I try the spaghetti, and it is to die for.

Angelo returns with a plate of lasagna for me and pork for Tony. He fills our wine glasses up yet again. I stare at Tony, straight into his blue eyes, and smile. He smiles back, and both of us start in on our meals. The lasagne is fabulous with thin noodles, ricotta, marinara sauce, sausage, and basil. Tony hasn't said a word since his meal arrived at the table. He is busy eating.

"How is the lasagna?" Tony asks as he finishes up his dinner.

"Great. I love it, along with all rest of the samples Angelo brought to me," I say. "Do you want dessert?" Tony asks.

"No. I'm not a big dessert fan." "How about a glass of port?"

"No, I'm not a big port fan either," I say.

"Coffee?" Tony asks.

"No. I only drink coffee in the morning," I say.

He looks at me with those big blue eyes like he's running out of things to offer. "Why don't we call it a night. I have to drive to East Marin."

"But I really enjoyed being with you tonight," Tony says.

"I enjoyed the entire evening—you, the food, the restaurant," I say.

Tony and I stand up to leave. Angelo sees us and catches up to us on the way out.

"Thanks, Angelo, we loved it," I say.

Tony and Angelo hug and slap backs again before we walk to the cars. Tony walks over to my car with me. I stand next to him, and he looks at me with those blue eyes and kisses me. I melt in my shoes, and he holds me tight. I'm very comfortable in his arms.

We kiss again, but I pull back and say, "I have to go."

Tony looks at me and says, "We will do this again soon."

I smile.

I drive to East Marin and pull into T's driveway. It's about 7 p.m.

It's windy and foggy. T isn't outside, so I knock on the door. T finally shows up at the front door.

"There you are," she says. "Everything OK?" T asks. I walk into the house, where it is a little warmer.

"I just came from an Italian restaurant in Larkspur named Bertelli's. I was with Tony Bertelli, who owns part of the joint," I say.

"*WHAT?* Who is Tony Bertelli?" T asks.

"He is the drywall foreman at the country club."
"And you're dating him?"
"This was the second time we got together. First for drinks and then this time for dinner. He is a tall, tan man with amazing blue eyes. Very attractive."
"Well, if you don't want him, I'll take him!" T says.

Chapter 25

Union Square in San Francisco is a fun place to shop. It's Saturday, and I decide to go into The City and do a little shopping. I park underground and walk up to the sidewalk. I pass Armani and Tiffany but make my way to Neiman Marcus and Macy's. The streets are crawling with people carrying shopping bags full of new clothes and shoes. The looks on their faces are looks of success like they just got a deal. I didn't think you could get a deal in Union Square. I only need a new pair of khakis, since I don't wear jeans at the job site at the country club, and a few new tops. I already have a new jacket from the pro shop, but if I see a sweater I like, I might buy that as well. T is visiting her parents today, so I'm on my own.

After an hour, I have everything I want and a few big bags to carry around. I do need to make one more stop. Gump's is just a few blocks off the square. It's a very exclusive store with an Asian flair and a modern American feel. I decide I want to look for cufflinks for Ben's birthday present. I go to the jewelry department. The first thing I think is *I can't afford anything here.*

The Country Club

They have cufflinks that top out at $3,000. I have the salesperson show me a few under $500, and I pick a black onyx pair for $350. I think Ben will like them, and I have them gift-wrapped from Gump's. He knows this place.

I drive back to East Marin and go straight to the yacht club. It's time for a glass of wine. I walk in, and the place is empty. I make my way to my favorite stool, second from the left, and settle myself.

Charles comes out from the back room. "Oh my, a customer! What is one to do?"

"Hi, Charles. Yes, please," I laugh. "How are you?"

Charles pours me a glass of zinfandel, brings it over to me, and parks himself right in front of me.

"What's new?" Charles asks, leaning to my side of the bar.

"Working, eating out a lot, went shopping in Union Square today. In fact, had dinner this week at an Italian restaurant in Larkspur called Bertelli's," I say.

"I've been there. It's very good," Charles shares.

"I went with one of the owners, a member of the Bertelli family," I state. "Really? How old was he, like ninety?" Charles asks.

I laugh. "No, his grandfather might be ninety, but Tony is thirty-six."

"I like the dive bar across the street, the Silver Peso." Charles grins. "Playing dominos tonight?" I ask.

"Hell yeah," Charles says. "Gino and I are looking for two more, so if you're in, that's good."

"I'm in. Where is everybody?"

"There's a club cruise to Sausalito today. Maybe that's it. No dinner on Saturday might be another reason. I'm just sitting behind the bar watching the A's game," Charles says.

There are no TVs in the club, but Charles has a four-inch screen TV he puts under the bar, so no one can see it but him.

"Yes, please." Charles pours me another glass of wine, and Joe Hunt walks in. He walks straight over to my stool and gives me a big hug before I can even stand up.

"Hi, darlin'," Joe says. "I haven't seen you in ages. Are you sailing at all? Charles, can I get a draft beer to go?"

"I'm not sailing much at all. Working, still living here in East Marin," I explain. "I'm here working on my boat and was thirsty," Joe says.

I smile. "It's good seeing you."

Joe grabs his beer and goes back to work.

"Well, that was fun. He was the second customer of the day," I say.

Charles just looks at me. "I like it when it's quiet."

"OK. I'll give you some quiet. What time should I be back for dominos?" I ask. "How about 7:30 p.m.," Charles says.

I drive to the triplex and pull into the driveway without opening the garage door since I'm leaving shortly to go back to the yacht club. I walk up the steps to the front porch, and there is a box from UPS sitting there. I unlock the door and push it open. I pick

The Country Club

up the box, which is rather light, and take it into the house. I slice it open with my X-Acto knife and find two golf head covers; one is a monkey, and the other is a cow. The card says, *Love, Ben,* of course. My driver and three wood have the original covers on them. I remember him asking me, when we were in Tahoe, why I don't have fun head covers. I never thought about it, but these will definitely brighten my bag.

The phone rings. "Hello?" I say.

"Hi, it's Ben."

"Hi, it's funny that you are calling now because I just opened up a package with the cutest golf head covers from you. Thank you!"

I smile. I could sense Ben was smiling over the phone. It's like he talks different when he's smiling.

"What are you doing?" Ben asks.

"Well, I went shopping in Union Square today, bought a few things. It was fun." "Who went with you?" Ben asks.

"I went by myself."

"What are you doing later?" Ben asks.

"Playing dominos at the yacht club." "Why?" Ben asks.

"That's what we do on Saturday nights when we have nothing else better to do," I explain.

"I'll call you next week," Ben says. "OK. Sounds good," I reply.

I hang up and leave the triplex for the yacht club. I pull up just as Gino arrives. We both get out of our cars at the same time, walk towards each other, and hug.

"I heard you were playing tonight!" Gino says. Gino is a single, retired engineer who I got to know through sailing and the yacht club. And playing dominos.

I smile as we both walk into the club. Charles is waiting for us, with a side table next to the bar, just in case we get a customer so he can get back there quickly and pretend he's still working.

"Yes, please," I say to Charles as soon as we walk in.

He already has Gino's gin and tonic, my wine, and his draft beer ready to go. We sit at the table and shuffle the dominos. We play Racehorse dominoes. Everyone picks a tile to see who starts. Highest tile goes first. Then, everyone takes eight tiles. However, this number can vary based on how many players are playing. The object of the game is to use all your tiles. If you cannot make a play, you must pick tiles from the boneyard until you can. A score is calculated on the perimeter tiles adding to a multiple of five. Playing a double or making a score plays again. Winner is the first to play all their tiles or go out. Scores for each player are the total remaining tiles after a player goes out. At the end of the evening, the player with the smallest number of points wins. The winner gets one dollar from the other players.

After three glasses of wine, four gin and tonics, and four draft beers, Gino is the big "wiener." Charles and I both give him a dollar for all his spectacular domino playing, and we pack the dominoes back in the box for next time.

Chapter 26

It's a warm September day. Members are at the club, golfing, lunching, and cocktailing. We are in our fourth week of overtime, and I'm getting tired.

Buzz walks into the office and says, "Is tonight a good night?"

"Yes." I smile

"I want to take you to a steakhouse in the financial district. Is that OK?" Buzz asks. My face lights up, and I say, "That's my favorite."

"We should drive separately and park just up the block in the alley," Buzz explains. "Are we going to Pub's?" I ask.

"Yes, have you ever been there?"

"No, but I heard it's great," I say. "H&S's office is just past the alley you are referring to, on California Street."

"We can meet at Pub's at 5 p.m. You don't have to change clothes. You look fine," Buzz says.

"I wasn't planning on changing clothes. I know that is a nice place, but this will have to work," I say.

I have on khakis and a button-down shirt. It's not like I have on jeans, a T-shirt, and work boots.

As I'm walking out of the job-site office, the phone rings.

"Hi, this is Loretta."

"Hi, this is Ben. Can I take you to dinner tonight?" Ben asks.

"Sorry, I have dinner plans."

I make my way down the hill to my car. No offers on a ride today. Maybe I'm a little late. It shouldn't take more than half an hour to get to the financial district. I'll park under the building in the alley. I leave the club at 4:30 p.m. I hope there's no traffic. The great highway turns into city streets that eventually turn into Bush, and that takes me one way, left on Kearny, right on California to the alley.

I pull into the parking garage, and Rich comes out of his little office and says, "I haven't seen you in a while."

I get out of my car and say, "I'm out off the great highway on a project." "Cool," Rich says.

"I'm going to Pub's for dinner," I say.

"I'll leave the car accessible with the keys in it," Rich explains.

"That works. It's good to see you." I smile as I walk out to the alley leading to California Street. Pub's is on the corner of California and Montgomery. I walk into the front door of Pub's at exactly 5 p.m. I tell the host I am meeting Dick Buzzy.

He immediately comes around from his podium and says, "Right this way, please."

I follow him into the dining room and find Buzz already sitting at the table. "Thank you," I say.

Buzz stands up as I approach the table and gives me a big hug and a kiss on the cheek. I smile and take my seat at the table.

"So, do they know you are here too?" I ask.

"Sort of. This is my go-to place in the financial district. After two visits, they get to know you and treat you like you are a regular," Buzz explains.

The waiter approaches the table with a pitcher of water, menus, and bread. "Thanks. Can we start with fried calamari and some drinks? What is your name?" Buzz asks.

"Yes, my name is Bobby, and what would you like to drink?" Buzz looks at me, and I say, "Yes, please."

"We'll take a glass of red zinfandel and a Manhattan," Buzz says. "I'll be right back with those," Bobby says.

I sit back and look at Buzz. He is tan and handsome tonight. "Have you been on vacation?" I ask. "You look tan and healthy."

"I took a trip to Arizona to play golf for a few days. It was very hot, but just what I needed," Buzz explains.

Bobby brings the drinks and the calamari.

"So, are you and Dick Little getting along any better?" Buzz asks.

"Oh, you mean little dick? The answer is no. Each week we talk about the trades we want—or should I say *need*—to authorize for overtime, but he does not take a leading role in these decisions. I'm expecting him to do that on behalf of the club. He seems like he's not interested in this project. He has a personal interest in the club, but only for himself. We'll summarize where we are at next week's committee meeting," I explain.

Bobby returns and asks if we are ready to order. Buzz looks at me, and I'm shaking my head yes.

"Yes," Buzz says. "Ladies first."

"I'll have a nine-ounce filet mignon, a baked potato, extra sour cream, and a side of cream corn."

Buzz says, "I'll have a veal porterhouse chop, skillet-fried potatoes, and a side of sautéed mushrooms and spinach. And another round of drinks, please."

Bobby smiles and leaves the table. I stare at Buzz, and he looks at me and smiles. "This is very nice. Thank you, Buzz," I say.

Buzz smiles.

Just as I look away from the table, I see Ben and a woman on his arm, walking into the restaurant to be seated. As they walk in, Ben recognizes me and comes over to the table.

"Hi, Loretta," Ben says. "What are you doing here?"

"Having dinner. Let me introduce you to Dick Buzzy, General Manager of the Golden Gate Club," I say. "Ben is a partner at CTS. We worked together on my last project."

Buzz stands and shakes Ben's hand. I was waiting for Ben to introduce his lady friend. She was smiling, listening to all the other introductions. When her introduction doesn't happen, I smile and say, "Enjoy your dinner," and they turn and start to walk to their table.

"Was that awkward, or was it just me?" Buzz asks. "He didn't even introduce her."

"No, it was awkward. Ben wants to have an affair with me, and I have so far refused. I thought he was going to hire me to work at CTS, but he thinks I should just have an affair with him. He will take care of me, and I won't have to work," I reveal.

"You've got to be kidding me. Here, I thought you were an intelligent, professional woman, and now I find out you have men throwing themselves at you," Buzz exclaims.

I laugh out loud. "Now, that's funny." I smile.

Bobby arrives with another round of drinks and a tray full of plates of food. He distributes the plates and says, "Dinner is served. Enjoy."

I try the cream corn first. Really good. Then I smash my baked potato with the sour cream. Awesome. I almost forgot about the steak. It's perfect. By this time, Buzz is halfway done with his chop and sides.

"Buzz, this is fantastic," I say as a loud pop, almost like a gunshot, resonates through the dining area.

We both look up, then at each other, and realize a truck had plowed through the storefront of the place. I huddle under Buzz's arm. There was no glass or debris flying where we were sitting. We try to finish our food. I take a large sip of wine to try and calm down as fire trucks and ambulances arrive to restore safety. I look up, and Ben is standing next to our table.

"Are you OK?" he asks.

Buzz looks at Ben with a look like, "She's fine. I'll take care of her, not you."

"We are sitting in the back, and you two are next to the windows. I just wanted to make sure you are OK," Ben explains.

"Thanks, Ben, but we're fine," I say.

Ben walks away, and Buzz turns and kisses me right at the table, like a cat claiming his territory.

"Wow, that was nice." I smile.

Buzz smiles and asks, "Are you finished? Let's blow this pop stand before the news crew gets here and starts interviewing patrons."

Chapter 27

It's Friday, and I'm glad it is. The weather is great, and it is harvest in the wine country. Harvest goes on for almost two months, depending on the varietal. Trailer trucks full of grapes drive up and down the highways, delivering grapes to the wineries to start the "crush." As I am dreaming about my first glass of zinfandel, Tony walks into the office. I smile because I haven't seen him in a few days.

"Hi, Loretta," Tony says. "I thought you might be gone by now, being it's Friday." "I'm surprised and happy to see you as well," I say.

"Well, since both of us are here, can I ask if you want to join me for happy hour at the Harbor Bar?" Tony asks.

"I'd love that." I smile.

"I'll meet you there in thirty minutes," Tony declares as he turns and walks out the door.

I finish up my last piece of paperwork for the week, pack up my bag, brush my hair, lock the office, and head on down the hill to my car. I wave to D as he heads home. It's getting to be quite comfortable working here. I pull out of the lot and make my way up the hill to the highway. The Harbor Bar is the next right off the highway. I park and go into the bar. The place is packed. It's definitely happy hour. Tony grabs my hand as soon as I walk in. We find a seat at the bar. A few of Tony's workers are here, as well as some electricians and painters. We are trying not to work overtime on the weekends, and we were successful in accomplishing the week's work, so we got to ditch Friday overtime as well. Maybe that's why some of these guys are here.

"What's your pleasure?" Tony asks.

It always makes my heart skip a beat when he says that. "Red wine; happy hour red is fine," I say.

The bartender brings over my wine. Tony has his beer.

"Cheers," I say as we clink glasses. "When you walked into the job-site office, I was thinking about wine country and harvest. It's such a fun time of year."

"Do you want to go wine tasting tomorrow?" Tony asks. "We can go up to Dry Creek Valley, taste for a few hours, and then come back to Bertelli's for an early dinner. Does that sound good?"

"Wow. Sounds great," I say as I wave to the bartender for another glass of wine.

He brings Tony another beer as well.

We talk a bit about the project and how frustrating some of the committee members can be. *I should say one committee member, not some.*

"I like working here," Tony says. "Even if Mel got caught selling golf balls in egg cartons." I laugh.

The Country Club

"He has tried that before, but not at a private club like this," Tony explains. "Do you golf?" I ask.

"Yes. Public courses. I can't afford to belong to private clubs like the Golden Gate Club," Tony says.

"Does Hard Drywall belong to a private club?" I ask.

"Of course. Hard Drywall belongs here. That is what keeps these private clubs going. It isn't the private membership; it's the corporate membership."

"Do you sail?" I ask. "No, do you?" Tony asks.

"I used to race around the bay. I still belong to the East Marin Yacht Club. We'll have to go there sometime," I say.

"So, how about I pick you up in East Marin at about noon?" Tony says.

"So, how about I cook you breakfast at 10:30 a.m., and we can leave at noon for the wine country?" I say

"That sounds even better," Tony says. "OK, so eggs over easy or scrambled?" "Scrambled."

"Sausage or bacon?" "Sausage."

"I'll take it from here," I say. "I'll see you at 10:30 a.m." "I do need to know where you live," Tony admits. "Oh, duh," I say. "I'm at 550 View Point Drive in East Marin. Off the freeway from the bridge, take Marine Street, straight up and over the hill, and turn left on View Point. It's a grey triplex on the right. My number is 701."

"Thanks. I'll see you tomorrow," Tony says.

We both left the bar at the same time, and I thought I wasn't going to get a hug, but I was not disappointed.

Tony walked me to my car, kissed me, and gave me a huge hug.

"Thanks," I say, as I get into the car and drive away. When I get to East Marin, I go straight to the market. I buy eggs, sausage, champagne, orange juice, and bread for toast. I'm in line, and I see Lisa. I sail with Lisa, and she lives here in East Marin as well.

"Hi, how are you?" Lisa asks.

"I'm great, just working a lot, not sailing a lot," I say.

"It was good to see you," Lisa says. "I'm going to stop and see Trisha today. It's been forever."

I head up the hill, pull into the garage, and lug the groceries up three flights of stairs. I put the groceries away and open a bottle of wine. I take a glass of wine onto the deck and relax. I'm very excited about Tony coming over tomorrow and the whole day we have planned. The phone rings, and I go inside to answer it.

'Hello?"

"Hi, it's Trish."

"Hey, what's up?" I ask.

"Lisa came by to say hi, and she said she saw you at the market and you were buying eggs."

I'm allergic to eggs. "Who is coming over?" teased T. *This is such a small town.*

"I'm making breakfast for Tony Bertelli tomorrow before we go wine tasting," I explain. "That sounds great. Maybe I can get to meet him," T says.

"You can come by and ask if you can borrow a cup of sugar," I laugh. "He'll be here at 10:30 a.m.," and I hang up the phone.

I go back onto the deck, sit down, and stare at the city. It's so spectacular…and the bridges. Wow. My favorite. I can't wait for tomorrow!

Chapter 28

There is no fog or wind this morning, and the sunlight is glistening on the bay. I shower and dress for a warm day. I pick capri pants and a tank top. Once I get upstairs, I see the sailboats making their way out on the bay. There must be a regatta. It's 9:30 a.m., and I don't need to prepare anything. The bread is ready for toast, the orange juice is ready for mimosas, the eggs are ready to be scrambled.

I hear a knock on the door. I open the door and see Ben.

"Come on in. You can't stay long. I have to leave at 10 a.m. to go to the wine country with T and Lisa."

"OK," Ben says.

"Like I told you before, you should call," I explain.

Ben makes his way to the front door. I open it up, and Tony is standing there. I invite Tony in.

"Who's that?" Ben asks.

"He is our chauffeur for this afternoon, or maybe I should say our designated driver."

"OK," Ben says as he walks down the steps to his car. "Have fun."

"What was that all about?" Tony asks.

"I'll tell you about it later. You're early, but that's OK. You found the place OK?" I ask.

"Yeah, I love it here. Look at all the sailboats on the bay." He smiles. "Can I get you a mimosa?" I ask.

"Sure, but only one. I'm driving," Tony says.

"What are you driving?" I ask.

"A Lexus 450," Tony replies.

"Oh, nice." I move to the kitchen to make the mimosas.

"I can't believe the view from this place," Tony says, as I hand him a mimosa. "Just relax, and I'll start breakfast," I say.

Tony sits down in the living room with the panoramic view. It's a delight. The sausages are cooking, and I'm scrambling the eggs. Toast isn't far behind.

"Tony, come sit at the table. Breakfast will be right up," I say.

Tony sits down, napkin in hand, and I deliver a breakfast plate to him. I go to get my plate, which is sausage and toast, and sit down at the table.

Tony looks at my plate and says, "No eggs?"

"No. I'm allergic to eggs. It's OK, though."

"Are you sure?" Tony asks.

"Absolutely."

Tony finishes his plate with ease. I take the last of my sausage and toast and finish as well.

"Why don't you go sit on the deck? I'll clean up, and we can go in like ten minutes," I say.

Suddenly, the doorbell rings. I walk to the door, open it up, and it's T with an empty cup of sugar.

"Come on in," I say. "I wasn't serious about the cup of sugar, you know."

The doorbell gets Tony back into the house, probably thinking this is what happens around here. Tony walks over to T and says, "Hi. I'm Tony."

T is mesmerized by his blue eyes and finally gets the air to say, "Hi, I'm Trisha." "Why don't you two get acquainted while I clean up the dishes," I say.

"So, where do you live?" T asks.

"I live in Marin," Tony says.

"And you work in The City?" T asks.

"No, I work where the jobs are. I work for Hard Drywall. We work all over. Where do you work?"

"I work for Wilder, Inc., a tech supply company in Santa Clara," T says. "OK. I'm done with the dishes, and I'm ready to go," I say.

Tony and T get up and walk toward the front door. I grab my purse, keys, and open the door. Everyone walks out, and I lock the front door. Tony and T start to walk down the steps.

"Bye, T," I say as she starts to walk up the street.

I'm right behind Tony, and he knows it. He opens the car door, and I get in. He gets in the other side, closes the door, and looks at me like that was a disaster.

"So, what was that all about?" Tony asks, as he starts the trek to Dry Creek Valley. "Here's the whole picture. Ben is a client that wants to have an affair with me. I have gone out to dinner with him, but I never agreed to have an affair with him. He showed up unexpectedly, and I told him I had to leave by 10 a.m., and then you showed up. I had no choice but to lie about the fact Lisa and T were going wine-tasting with me and that you were our chauffeur. Or should I say our designated driver?"

"And then Trisha arrived," Tony says, "and I wondered what she was doing."

"She wanted to meet you. She knew you were coming to breakfast because everyone knew I bought eggs at the market."

Tony laughs.

"This is a small town; welcome to it."

"So, what wineries do you want to taste at?" Tony asks. "I like Wilson," I say.

"Any others?" Tony asks.

"How about Ferrari-Carano and Seghesio?" I suggest.

"Sounds good to me," Tony says.

We drive up the freeway in Tony's car and pull off at the Healdsburg exit to go to Seghesio. This winery is old and family owned. They renovated the place a few years ago, and it's beautiful.

"I'm glad we stopped here. I worked on this project." He smiles. "Wow. Well, I'm glad we stopped too."

We walk in through double, half-arched doors into this twenty-foot-high room with a large bar running down the back wall. We belly up to it and are greeted by a fellow named Sam. Sam pours us five kinds of zinfandel, but they all taste the same. Maybe it's because I just brushed my teeth.

We head to Ferrari-Carano. It's at the almost very end of Dry Creek Road. I like this winery for the gardens. They plant four thousand tulips each spring, and the overall grounds are very nice. We park and start meandering through the gardens. Thirty minutes later, we find our way to the tasting room. They ask if we want to start with whites.

"Red, please," I say.

They only have a zinfandel and a Cabernet Sauvignon, but that will be good for my designated driver to only have two tastes before we go to Wilson. We are served the two tastes; maybe that's why they focus on their white wines.

We thank the server and make our way back through the garden to the parking lot. At the car, I ask Tony, "Did you like the gardens?"

"They were as beautiful as you are," Tony reveals. He throws his arms around me and kisses me. My knees want to fold.

"Thanks for such a great day." I smile.

"It's not over yet," Tony explains. "We have a couple more stops."

We get into the car and head to Wilson. We finally find a parking spot and make our way to the tasting room. The place is packed. We squeeze our way to the bar and ask for two glasses.

"Hi, I'm Stella. I'll be serving you today."

She sets down the glasses and pours the first wine, which is a Sauvignon Blanc, which is very grapefruit forward. Tony and I taste and agree. Next is a chardonnay in oak barrels for two years. It has a sweet vanilla finish. We taste. We are ready for some reds. As she pours a taste into our glasses, Stella says the zinfandel is dark and smoky, with a pepper finish. Tony and I taste and really like this one. The next one is a malbec; not too dry, not too fruity. We like it. And finally, Stella pours a Cabernet Sauvignon. We taste, and both really like it.

We leave Wilson with a purchase of one bottle of zinfandel. Once we are in the car, Tony asks, "Did you enjoy that?"

"I loved it," I state. "Most guys don't really like wine tasting. They would rather drink beer at the pub, watching the game."

"I like that too, but I like spending the day with you." Tony smiles.

It's 3:30 p.m., and we are headed down the freeway to Bertelli's. We pull into the parking lot at 4:15 p.m. and get out of the car. Tony walks over to me and gives me a hand to stand and exit the car. We both walk into the restaurant, and there is no one there. Finally, Tony's brother Angelo comes in and asks where we've been all day.

"Wine tasting. We brought in the bottle we bought to drink with our dinner today," Tony says.

"Do you want me to uncork it for you now?" Angelo asks.

"Yes, bro, we'll be at my favorite table."

Angelo comes over to Tony, and they backslap each other before he takes the bottle of wine. We make our way to his favorite table and take a seat.

"Why is this your favorite table?" I ask. There doesn't seem to be anything special about it.

"When I was a toddler, my parents brought me to work with them and sat me at this table. I just played with my cars and army men. Once the rush was over, my mom and I would go home, and she'd put me to bed," Tony explains.

I smile.

Angelo returns with two glasses and the bottle of wine that we bought today. He uncorks it and pours a sip for Tony to taste, just to make sure it's not bad. Tony takes a sip and nods his head in favor. Angelo then proceeds to fill the glasses.

"Cheers," I say as we both raise our glasses and clink them together.

"So, you're going to be off the project in a few weeks. Do you know where your next project is?" I ask.

"Unfortunately, it's at my ex-wife's house," Tony claims. "What? Why?" I ask.

"It's a long story, but we have a long time. Hard Drywall is an employee-owned corporation, and we get company stock in addition to our union benefits. When we got divorced, she wanted out because she found someone else to carry on with. So, the lawyer offered the house, half of my company stock at the time, no more union benefits, no Bertelli ownership, and alimony. That ended if she remarried. They accepted the deal. Unbeknownst to her, my stock kept building, and the union had a retirement plan that we didn't include in the divorce settlement. To make things even better for me, she remarried six months after the divorce, so the alimony stopped."

Angelo brings over some calamari and fills our glasses. We both smile at him.

"It sounds like she didn't have a good lawyer," I say.

The Country Club

"She wanted out and would have agreed to anything," Tony says. "It wasn't because of you?" I ask.

"Oh, no. I did love my wife, but she had other plans and ideas. As it turns out, her new marriage didn't last a year. So, it's a few years later, and she is struggling to pay the bills, only works part time. The good news is I rarely hear from her unless she needs work around the house," Tony admits.

Angelo is heading our way with plates full of spaghetti and meatballs and pork Milanese.

"Would you like grated cheese?" "Yes, please," I say.

We both dig in and start eating. Angelo brings another bottle of wine since we finished the one that we bought in the wine country. The food here is great, and a few more customers stroll in.

"I'm stuffed," I say as I finish my plate.

"Me too," Tony says. "If we can't finish the second bottle, they can recork it and put it in a brown paper bag, and we can finish it at your house."

"I'm fine with that," I say.

Angelo comes to the table and says, "No coffee or dessert today?" "No thank you. We have had a long day," I say.

Tony hands Angelo the half-finished bottle of wine, and Angelo hands Tony something to sign. I don't know if he pays for meals here or not. Angelo returns with a brown paper bag. Tony stands up and gives his brother a hug and a few backslaps. I'm glad Tony doesn't backslap me, although I heard it's a sign of affection, maybe only for guys.

We walk to the car. Tony opens my door for me, but before I get in, I stand real close to him and say, "Thanks for the great day," and then kiss him and hop in the car.

"You're welcome," Tony says as he walks around to the driver's side and gets in. We leave the parking lot, merge onto the highway and then the bridge, and head over the bay to East Marin.

"You remember how to get there?" I ask.

"Yes, I was just there this morning," Tony states. "I just wonder how many people are going to show up when we get there."

I laugh. We pull into the driveway and walk up the steps. I unlock the door, push it open, and all you see is the bay and the city and the bridges. We both walk in and stop to take in the view. Then he grabs me around the waist and kisses me. I don't resist. Tony forgot the wine in the car, so when he runs back to the car, I get two wine glasses out. When he returns, I uncork the bottle again.

I fill up our glasses, hand him his, and say, "Let's sit on the balcony. It's more like a perch than a balcony, and it's only big enough for two chairs. It's a warm, beautiful evening."

Tony's eyes look bluer with the bay reflecting on them. I stare at him; he smiles. And then we both stare at the city and the bay. We even get a sunset. Once the sun goes down, Tony says, "I better go. Tomorrow is a workday."

"No, it's not. Not on my project," I insist.

"I know, but I work at the restaurant on Sundays and give my mom and dad the day off," Tony explains.

"Where did I find you? That's awfully nice of you. I thought all the nice guys were taken." I smile.

"You remember where you found me when one of my guys was selling golf balls in egg cartons to the members?"

Tony laughs as he stands and holds my hands to help me up.

"I remember," I admit.

Suddenly, I am surrounded by strong arms and a kiss to send me to the moon. We walk to the front door and say goodbye. I may smile all night.

Chapter 29

The tenth committee meeting is about to start. Buzz opens the meeting and says, "We made it this far, but we still have a couple of months to go. Loretta, can you give us an update?"

"Yes, the carpet and lockers are on track to be here October 1st. The men's locker room is almost complete in the spa and shower area. The painters are on schedule with painting and stenciling the beams. The electricians and plumbers may need to do some overtime to make the date. I'll calculate what that cost might be and discuss it at our weekly meeting. The overtime that is already approved is $175,000."

"No way," Dick Little says.

"Yes way. You approved $175,000 in overtime at our weekly meeting," I explain. "That's wrong," Dick says.

"No, that's right," I say. "The weekly meetings that approve the overtime are being tallied for the committee meetings. That's where the $175,000 comes from. Did the committee give Dick Little authorization to approve the overtime costs?" I ask.

The Country Club

"Yes," Dick Buzzy says.

"So, if overtime is or was approved on a weekly basis, it is approved," I conclude. "Not necessarily," Dick Little says.

"What do you mean?"

"Approval and payment are two different things," Dick Little says.

"I would agree with what you're saying, but the only difference is if the work is in place or not. Approval for 'not in place' does not constitute payment. You, on the other hand, approve the overtime, so the subs proceed, and as soon as the work is done, reject the cost. I have submitted progress payments that include the overtime for our subcontractors," I say.

"And I have rejected them," Dick Little says.

"What?" I ask. "How can you approve the overtime and then reject the cost?" "Does anyone else on the committee have an opinion on what is going on?" Buzz asks.

"We approved the overtime costs, and we should approve the payments," Dick the architect says.

"All we're trying to do is get to the November 8th date, and if we all can't commit to getting there, then I don't know how to manage this project," I explain.

"Let's move on," Buzz says. "Is there any other business to discuss at today's meeting?"

"I heard there was somebody selling golf balls in egg cartons at the entry to the club. Is that true?" Dick the engineer asks.

"Yes, but I met with the pro—Wayne at the pro shop—and we closed him out of the business of selling golf balls at a private club," I say.

"I have an invoice for $12,000 for the cast stone mantel that is installed. Can I give it to you, Loretta, and H&S can pay them?" Dick Little explains.

"No, you can't. The cast stone mantel is NIC—not in contract," I say. "But you can still pay the invoice," Dick Little says.

"I would have to submit a change order, and I have a funny suspicion that you would reject it," I say.

"I would never do that," Dick Little says.

"You've done it before on the concrete slab in the kitchen and the overtime costs.

Why would I believe you now?" I ask.

"For Christ's sake," Buzz pipes up. "Loretta, just submit a change order for the mantel, include it in your next pay application, and we will pay you."

"Thank you," I say.

I still have a tour at 1 p.m. to guide. "Is anyone joining me on the tour today?" I ask.

D says, "There are eighteen members signed up for the tour."

Buzz says, "I'll join you, Loretta."

"Thanks. Anyone else?" No reply.

It's almost like members sneak in when no one is around, and the committee knows exactly what's going on, and they don't have to go on these silly tours.

So, at 12:55 p.m., I drag the box of hard hats out to the hallway, step outside to the driveway, and wait for the members to congregate. When I think I count eighteen members, plus Buzz, I smile and say, "Welcome. If everyone could go into the hallway, grab a hard hat, and meet in the garden room, that would be perfect."

Buzz walks up to me and smiles. This is good PR for the club, and he hears the positive response from the members from the tours all the time.

We all gather in the garden room. "Good afternoon. I'm Loretta Novak, project manager for H&S. I will walk you through the progress we are making on the construction. Please stay together and don't wander off."

"Here, in the garden room, the ceiling is being replaced with glass panels," I say.

We move toward the main entry. The hardwood floor and wood stairs are being installed, so we must go around to the back bar and lounge. We work our way around the construction and end up in the main bar. Covered wood beams are being installed, so we continue into the kitchen, where only electrical and plumbing are going on, waiting for the delivery of the kitchen equipment, which is four weeks out. We make it back to the lobby and down the stairs, with a stop at the new ladies' locker room. Next is the men's locker room. Lockers are still four weeks out as well, so the room is big and empty now. The bathroom, shower, and spa are being finished as we make our way through. We head out of the locker room and up the steps outside to the driveway.

"Thanks, everybody. Please put your hard hats in the box and have a nice day," I say.

Buzz comes over to me and smiles even bigger. "You do such a great job at these tours. Thanks."

"You're welcome. Thanks for bringing sanity to the meeting this morning," I say.

"Are you ready for happy hour?" Buzz asks.

"Yes, I am. Dick Little gets me going. I don't know how you deal with him," I state.

Completely ignoring my comment, Buzz says, "I'll come and take you to your car in thirty minutes, and you can drive up and park it in the circle. I'll let D know."

I went back to my desk and organized things for tomorrow. The phone rings. "Hi, this is Loretta."

"Hi, this is Ben."

"Hi, Ben. I'm leaving the office right now, so I don't have time to talk," I say.

"Can I buy you a drink tonight?" Ben asks.

"No, I'm busy. I'll talk to you later," I say and hang up the phone.

I lock up the office and walk out to the circle to find Buzz sitting in his car, waiting for me. I smile, jumping into his car.

"Hi," Buzz says, as he makes his way down to my car. I jump out, jump into my car, and make my way up the road with Buzz behind me. I park my car in the circle, jump out, and jump into his car.

"Hi! Where are we going?" I ask.

"Do you just want to go to the Harbor Bar?" Buzz asks.

"That's fine. But if that's the case, I will drive myself. It's on my way home."

"OK," Buzz says. "I'll meet you there."

I jump out of his car, into my car, and follow Buzz. Buzz turns out of the driveway to the road. We both turn right and an almost immediate right to get to the Harbor Bar. We both park, and we walk to the bar, holding hands. He opens the door. We walk in and find two seats at the bar.

The bartender walks our way and asks, "What can I get you two?"

"I'll take a red zinfandel," I say.

"I'll take a gin and tonic," Buzz says.

Buzz grabs my hand and smiles. I look into his gorgeous green eyes and smile. The drinks are delivered finally, and Buzz distracts me.

"What are you going to do with Dick Little?" I ask. "What do you mean?" Buzz asks.

"I mean, he is ruining this project for me," I say. "I just don't want to operate like him."

"Frankly, neither do I," Buzz says after taking a sip of his drink. "But I didn't hire him, the committee did."

"But he works for you," I state.

"No, not technically. He works for the committee. After each meeting, you go back to work, and we review and approve or reject Dick Little's monthly invoice, incidentals, and vendor invoices he may have," Buzz explains.

"But why did he want me to pay for the $12,000 stone mantel? So he could reject my change order for it and deny payment?" I ask.

Buzz laughs. "You're very cute when you're angry."

I blush and smile at him. "Let's change the subject. So, are you taking vacation anytime soon?" I ask.

"Actually, I am. I'm going on a golf trip to Arizona in the first week of October. I still have a few golfing buddies who live there. We get together every year. How 'bout you?" Buzz asks.

"No, maybe once the project is complete and the members move back in, I can relax," I admit.

We order another round, and who walks into the bar but Tony Bertelli. This is almost as bad as Tony showing up at my place and Ben being there. Tony finally notices me at the bar, and he approaches Buzz and me.

"Hi, Tony, good to see you," I say before he has a chance to hug me. "Tony, this is Dick Buzzy, General Manager of the Golden Gate Club. Dick, this is Tony Bertelli, Drywall foreman for Hard Drywall on the project," I explain as they shake hands.

"I better go back with my crew. Nice to meet you, Dick, and I'll see you soon, Loretta," Tony says and walks away. "He's friendly," Buzz says.

"Yeah, I met Tony on the site after Wayne and I shut down the guy selling golf balls in egg cartons. That guy works for Hard Drywall as well," I say.

Buzz laughs. "It's always something." Buzz looks at his watch and says, "I've got to go. I'm getting my hair cut, and I completely forgot about it."

"Don't worry, just go. I got the check, and I have my car. Just go," I say.

"Are you sure?" Buzz asks.

"You'll owe me big time, but that's all," I say.

The Country Club

Buzz gives me a kiss on the cheek and runs out the door. I still have half a glass of wine, and I see Tony walking over.

"Did you scare him away?" Tony laughs.

I smile and say, "No, he forgot a commitment he has."

"Good, you can come over and join me at our table," Tony says. I was hoping he'd say that. I grab my wine and my purse and pay the bar tab.

"And he even made you pay?" Tony jokes.

"He is my client. I can pay for a few drinks at a fancy place like this," I proclaim. We walk over to the table. There are four others sitting there.

"Guys, this is Loretta, the project manager for the GC on our project," Tony says.

We sit down, and Tony orders another round. I recognize Mel from the golf-ball-selling situation, but no one else.

"I'm not sure I need another drink," I say.

"It's OK. I'll follow you home if I have to." Tony smiles.

"Well, if you are going to follow me home, let's go right now," I say. "OK. Bye, guys. I'll catch you in the morning," Tony says.

Tony and I walk out of the bar. He gets me to my car and hugs and kisses me.

"I miss you," Tony says. "I'm glad I ran into you here. Let's go to your house, order a pizza, and stare at the city lights."

"Sounds good. I'll take the lead," I say.

We both get in our vehicles, make our way out of the parking lot, across the Golden Gate Bridge, and across the San Rafael Bridge to East Marin.

I pull into the driveway. I don't have an automatic opener, so I have to stop, get out of my car and pull the garage door open, get back in my car, and pull the car into the garage.

Tony pulls into the driveway as soon as I pull the car into the garage.

"We can come up this way," I say, as I direct Tony to follow me up the steps. After three flights, we get to the top and the view.

"Wow, I think I say this every time I come here."
"You've only been here once," I say.

Tony makes his way outside. I ask if I can get him something.

"What kind of beer do you have?" Tony asks, as he walks back inside. "Heineken."

"That's it?" Tony asks.

"Yes, that's the only beer I drink."

"Well, I guess I'll have a Heineken," Tony says. "What are you going to have?"

I open the beer and hand it to Tony, and say, "I'm going to open a bottle of wine and order the pizza. What kind of pizza do you like?" I ask.

"Pepperoni and sausage," Tony claims. "Is that OK with you?"

"My favorite is Hawaiian. I'll get half of each," I say.

Tony walks back outside. I call the pizza delivery, open a bottle of wine, pour a glass, and join Tony on the deck.

The Country Club

"So, how is the restaurant doing?" I ask.

"It's doing great. My mom and dad like their family chipping in and working at the store and restaurant," Tony explains.

"Where is the Bertelli store?" I ask.

"It's in Larkspur shopping center," Tony answers.

"I'm familiar with that place," I say.

Twenty minutes later, the doorbell rings, and I go to answer it.

"Hi."

"Here's your pizza."

I take the pizza inside, grab my credit card, and walk back to the front porch. The delivery person runs my credit card through the machine, and I'm good to go. I move the pizza to the dining room table along with plates and napkins, and I call Tony to come and eat.

"I could sit out there all day long," Tony says as he sits downs and helps himself to a piece of pizza. "Can I get you a piece?"

"Sure," I say as I smile. "Another beer?"

"Sure," Tony says.

I come back with the beer, and we start eating. We eat the entire pizza. I clear the table, and we both head back to the deck to watch the sunset. We sit very close together, holding hands and staring at the view.

"I probably should go soon," Tony says as he stands. "Tomorrow is an early workday."

"You can stay if you want." I smile.

Tony walks towards me, grabs my hands, and pulls me up to stand. He kisses me, and my insides shiver. He pulls back and looks into my eyes.

"I would like to stay, but we both know what might happen if I do," Tony says. "Let's just take things slow."

"But—"

"But nothing," Tony says as he heads for the door, turns, and kisses me goodbye. I stand in the doorway and watch him leave.

Chapter 30

Ben's birthday is September 4th. The last time I talked with him, I asked him if we could celebrate and he said to invite anyone I'd like. I make sure Ben is available a few days after his birthday. Friday, September 6th, works best. Carroll and Drew are both available that day too. So now all I have to do is figure out where to go. We can go to the Tadich Grill, but that's more of a lunch and dinner place, and we are just having drinks. We can go the Boon Docks, but that's more of a dive. But how about Pier 23? It is on the Embarcadero, with great views of the bay, and it has a funky, rustic feel to it. I call Ben, Carroll, and Drew to let them know the plan. I pick 4 p.m. because it is a Friday. I call Pier 23 and reserve a table for 4 p.m. on the deck. I just hope it's not too windy and cold.

The day before, I get Ben's present out of the bag, and it's already gift-wrapped, so I can't even look at them again before I give them to him. I think I remember they were nice. Oh no, I didn't get a card. I find a notecard and write *Happy Birthday Ben* and attach it to the box. It will be fine. I head to the country club.

Fridays are pretty slow, but there is a lot of activity on the project. We had no approved overtime today, or this weekend, so that will give the guys a break. I'm sitting at my desk, cleaning up my desk, and Tony walks in.

"Can I buy you a drink at happy hour?" Tony asks.

"Sorry, I already have plans," I say.

He just looks at me with those blue eyes and asks, "I can't talk you out of it?" "No, but you can talk me into a happy hour next week." I smile.

"Perfect," Tony says as he walks out of the office.

At 3:30 p.m., I close the office and start walking down the hill to my car, and Buzz stops in his golf cart. I get in.

"Hi, can I interest you in a cocktail tonight?" Buzz asks.

"No, I have plans," I say as he drops me off at my car. "Maybe next week," I say.

"Thanks for the ride." I kiss him on the cheek and jump out of the golf cart and into my Miata and drive to Pier 23. Parking sucks around that area of the Embarcadero, but I find a small parking lot on the pier next to Pier 23 that is inexpensive. I walk into the restaurant and ask for our reservations. The maître d' walks me out to the deck overlooking the bay. It was warm, with no wind, and fabulous.

Five minutes later, I see the other three moving my way. I stand up as they approach the table.

"Hi," I say as I give them all hugs and kisses. "Have a seat because we're here for a good time, not a long time."

They all laugh, and the waiter makes his way to our table. "What can I get for everyone?"

"An Absolut over with an olive, a glass of red zinfandel, a draft beer, and a Manhattan," Ben says.

"So, how is married life, Drew?" I ask. "So far, so good," Drew says.

"What is your wife's name?" I ask. "Jennifer."

The waiter delivers the drinks, and I ask if we can see a happy hour menu. I don't know if everyone wants a snack or not.

"So, Ben, how old did you turn on your birthday?" I ask. "Thirty-six."

"I will be thirty-six in November," I say.

We look at the menu and decide on some fried calamari. The waiter stops by, and we get another round and the calamari.

"Carroll, how are you doing?" I ask.

"I'm fine. I'm old and tired, but I'm fine." "That's good," I say, shaking my head and smiling.

The calamari and drinks are delivered to the table, and we start snacking. I pull the present out of my purse and hand it to Ben.

"What's this?" Ben asks.

"It's your birthday present," I say.

"You shouldn't have bought me a birthday present," Ben says. "But I did," I say. "Open it up."

Ben proceeds to open the card. He knew it was from me. He starts to unwrap the gift. I can tell he already recognizes the Gump's gift wrap. He rips the wrapping off the box and opens the box to find onyx cufflinks.

"Oh my god, they're beautiful!" Ben smiles.

"I'm glad you like them," I say. "Just what you need is another pair of cufflinks, but oh well then."

"No woman has ever bought me such a nice gift," Ben reflects.

We all finish our drinks, and Carroll pays the bill. We all stand to leave. "This was great, Loretta," Ben says.

"I'm glad you enjoyed yourself," I say.

"I love my cufflinks," Ben admits.

"I'm glad you do."

We all exit the deck, through the restaurant, and onto the Embarcadero. We have hugs and kisses for everybody before they make their way to their cars. Ben walks me to my car in the parking lot.

"Thanks for the cufflinks. I like them so much," Ben says. I smile. He kisses me, and I don't resist.

"Does this mean you are ready to have an affair with me?" Ben asks.

"No, Ben, it means that I like you and you're a good friend, but it doesn't mean that I love you and I want to have an affair with you," I explain.

Ben looks at me with a face like a boy who didn't get the toy he wanted for Christmas. I don't know what to say to him. I get in the Miata and drive away.

I see T's car as I drive down our street. I stop and get out. I haven't seen T for a while. T opens the door, comes out, and gives me a big hug.

"You haven't been here forever. Come on in," T says.

The Country Club

"I've been busy. So many men. So little time," I joke.

We both laugh as T pours a glass of wine for each of us. We sit down at the window and take in the view.

"So, where have you been?" T asks.

"Well, tonight I celebrated Ben's birthday with drinks at Pier 23. Carroll and Drew came, and it was the perfect day on the bay. I bought Ben onyx cufflinks from Gump's for his birthday."

"WHAT!" T screams. "Cufflinks? I didn't think anyone wore cufflinks anymore. Even my father doesn't wear cufflinks."

"How is your father?" I ask.

"Not good. The diabetes is catching up with him," T explains. "Actually, I don't know how much longer he has."

"Oh, T, oh my, are you OK?" I ask.

"I'll be fine. My family is used to the trouble my father went through with diabetes," T says.

"Is he still working?" I ask.

"No. His business partner and I are running the business now," T says.

"And is that OK?" I ask.

"It has to be OK," T explains.

"I love your attitude." I smile.

"So, what else has been going on?" T asks.

"On Tuesday, after my committee meeting and job-site tour, I ended up at happy hour with Buzz. He's the general manager of the Golden Gate Club. We golfed together and have had dinner and drinks a few times. We went to a small bar close to the club.

He forgot he had a haircut that afternoon, so he ran off, but Tony was there, so Tony and I came back to East Marin to eat pizza and watch the sunset."

"And?" T asks.

"I asked him to stay, but he wants to take it slow, so he left," I say. "Wow," T says.

"Are you dating anyone?" I ask.

"No, not now. There must be something wrong with me. You're hanging out with three guys, and I got nothing," T says.

"There is nothing wrong with you, sweetie," I say. "You just aren't in the right guy arena. Think about it. You know all the guys who sail and all the guys who work in the Spacely Sprockets business. That's a lot of guys.

"I, on the other hand, know all the guys who sail, know all the guys who work in construction, know all the guys who golf, and know all the guys who manage companies H&S works for. That's gotta be 100,000 guys, and I still think it's amazing that three of them want to spend time with me."

Chapter 31

T calls me at work, which is not like her.

I answer. "Hi, T. What's going on?"

"My dad died this morning," T says, with tears in her eyes.

"Oh my, I'm so sorry. What can I do to help you and your family?" I ask.

"Well, there is not much to do. My dad is being cremated, and my mom is sponsoring a celebration of life in a couple days."

"OK," I say. "Then, what do you need?"

"I just want you to be with me through this," T says.

"I'm in," I say.

I'm at work and trying to start my day, but I can't stop thinking about T and the construction schedule. The carpet arrived today, the painters are working in all rooms, and all the renovated light fixtures are being installed.

I look up from my desk, and the electrical foremen with Sun Electric and the electrical inspector walk into the project office. "Hi, I'm Inspector Duffy, and I am new to the project."

"And I'm Cal, with Sun Electric."

Bill gets up and says, "Hi, I'm Bill, superintendent on this job site, and this is Loretta Novak, project manager."

"Nice to meet both of you," Inspector Duffy says. "Well, there is a problem with the distribution panel, and it will need to be replaced."

Bill looks at the electrical foremen and asks, "This is not in our original scope of work?"

"No, this is a new requirement from the inspector," Cal says.

Cal is a tall, blond, tan, and athletic-looking guy, and I am completely mesmerized by him. All I need is a fourth guy to hang out with.

"So, what are we talking about here?"

"Well, the panel probably has a four to six-week lead time. It will take a week to install, so that puts us at mid-November," Cal explains.

"That's not going to work. Can you get me a price and an extra to expedite it? We need to get the final inspection the first week of November," I explain.

"I'll get back to you this afternoon," Cal says.

"That's perfect. I can get approval today, and we can order tomorrow."

Cal comes back to the job-site office at 2 p.m. "Hi, Loretta. I have the pricing. The new panel is five thousand. To expedite the delivery is another grand. Cost to install is another four grand."

"OK," I say. "So, ten grand total. Thanks. Can I call you later when I get it approved?"

"I'll just stop back before I leave today," Cal says. I call Buzz.

"This is Dick Buzzy. Can I help you?"

"This is Loretta."

"Are you OK?" Buzz asks. "You never call me."

"I know, but I have a pressing issue. The electrical inspector said the existing distribution panel does not meet code and needs to be replaced. It will cost about ten grand. We must buy it tomorrow in order to make the November date. I don't know if we can get the committee together this afternoon and authorize H&S to proceed or not," I explain.

"That's not going to happen, but you have to call Dick Little," Buzz states. "Can't you call him? He hates me," I say.

"OK, let's do this. Proceed with the purchase of the panel and submit a change order for ten thousand. I will get this to the committee before the last committee meeting on October 29th."

"I can fax the change order first thing tomorrow morning. Thanks, Buzz." I smile. "You're welcome."

An hour later, Cal walks into the job-site office. I look up and smile. "Go ahead and place the order, expedited. Just confirm the delivery date and get that to me," I say. "If you need something in writing, I can get it to you tomorrow morning."

"That's fine," Cal says. "So, can I buy you a drink? You look stressed."

"Sure, that would be nice." I smile. "I'll meet you at the Harbor Bar in an hour." "Works for me," Cal says.

The most important thing I can do as a project manager is develop a relationship with the subcontractors.

I lock the office and walk to my car. No offers for rides today. I jump in the Miata and see a note on the windshield. I get halfway out and pull the note from under the windshield wiper. The note reads, *Can't stop thinking about you. Tony.*

I smile and get back in my car and drive to Harbor Bar. I don't see any Sun Electric or Hard Drywall trucks. Coast is clear.

I make my way to the bar, find a seat, and think about T. She was very close to her dad, and I hope she is holding up OK.

"Hello, is anybody in there?" Cal jokes. "I walked up, and you were definitely somewhere else."

"Hi, I'm sorry. I'm back now. Have a seat," I say as I wave the bartender over. "I know you'll have a red zinfandel, and what can I get you, sir?"

Barry asks. "I'll have a Coors Light draft."

"Do you come here often?" Cal asks.

"That's the oldest pickup line ever," I laugh.

"Well, he knew what you drink. I just thought you might come here often," Cal says.

"A good bartender will remember what you drink after the first visit. He might not remember your name, but he remembers what you drink. On a project like this, we do come here often. Thanks for inviting me for a drink, so I don't have to drink alone. Short of the electrical inspector surprise, my best friend's father died today, so that's why I'm a little stressed out."

"So, tell me a little about Cal, starting with your last name," I say.

"My full name is Calvin Davis. I am divorced and live in The City." *Is every man alive over thirty and divorced?* "I have worked for Sun Electric for fifteen years, since I was eighteen."

"That means you're thirty-three. Do you want to guess how old I am?" I ask.

"Don't do this to me. Just tell me," Cal says.

"I'm thirty-five."

"Thanks. Women have a thing with age," Cal says. "I'm not like most women," I admit.

"I'm starting to realize that," Cal laughs. We order another round and ask for the check.

"So, you decided to be an electrician instead of going to college. That's great," I say. "I'm doing just fine being an electrical foreman with no college payments."

"How long have you been divorced?" I ask.

"Ten years. I was young and dumb, and she was younger and dumber," Cal says. I laugh. "As long as you're still not paying for being young and dumb," I say. "No, I'm good."

The new drinks are served with the check. I throw my credit card out. Cal grabs my hand and says, "I've got this. Well, Sun Electric's got this," Cal says.

"OK. Thanks," I say as I grab my card from the bar. "What part of The City do you live in?" I ask.

"The Marina. I'm a social member at the Golden Gate Yacht Club, but I don't sail," Cal explains.

"I'm a member of the East Marin Yacht Club and used to race a lot in the bay," I say.

"Sounds like fun. How did you land a project manager's position at H&S?" Cal asks.

"Well, I have a civil engineering degree, and you can do just about anything with that," I say.

"Like being an electrician?" Cal asks.

"No. I never understood the electrical side of things. Even today, the distribution panel is not something I understand. I can pay to purchase it and get it installed, but that doesn't mean I understand exactly what it is," I explain.

We finish our drinks and look at each other like we got to know each other a bit better.

"Would it be OK if I asked you out again?" Cal asks.

"Sure, I'd like that." *The most important thing I can do as a project manager is develop a relationship with the subcontractors.* "But it's going to be crazy busy to finish this project. Sounds like you are going to be here to the bitter end with me," I say.

"Yes, I am."

Chapter 32

The month of October is expected to be busy, and everyone is slammed. The kitchen equipment is being installed. The lockers arrived yesterday. The carpet is being installed. The sub's crew sizes have doubled since September to ensure we make the end date of Nov 8th. I got the change order off to Cal and Buzz for the distribution panel. Cal said even with expediting, the panel wouldn't arrive until October 29th. That would allow for one week of installation, but that would be cutting it close. I grab my hard hat and walk the entire job site. Painters, millworkers, plumbers, electricians. There must be 150 workers here. I like that the subs stepped it up with manpower. Now is not the time for overtime. We need to keep the quality high at the end of the project like this. Sometimes, overtime can get a little sloppy because the crews are working long hours.

I go back to the job-site office and settle into a day of paperwork, submitting a pay app for September, and signing subcontractor invoices for payment. Once I went through the invoices, the H&S pay app included $70,000 in overtime expenses. August's pay app had the remainder of the overtime, which is $40,000, and I'm not anticipating any overtime in October. We might need a little, but not with the size of these crews. H&S has not been paid for August, but it's due now. I tally September's pay app at $875,000.

It's 3 p.m., and I'm ready for a break. Bill walks in with the mail, turns around, and says, "See you tomorrow, Loretta." Bill rarely stays at the job site after 3 p.m. I don't know what time he gets here in the morning because he's always here when I show up. I go through the mail and see an envelope from Golden Gate Town and Country Club addressed to me. I open it, and it's a letter from Dick Little. It reads:

To: Loretta Novak From: Dick Little

Date: October 12, 1996

The committee for the renovation of the Golden Gate Town and Country Club project has made a decision to not reimburse H&S or its subcontractors for any overtime spent on this project. We made this decision due to the fact that H&S never formally requested a delay to the project. According to your contract, costs associated with delays to the schedule must be submitted in writing to the committee.

I can feel I'm about to explode in anger. When I'm really angry, I cry. I read the letter again as tears start running down my cheeks. I can't believe Dick Little called me on the exact thing he wouldn't allow. A delay. We talked about these things, and I tried to be cooperative and accommodating to their needs while still building the project. We talked about overtime every week. We discussed it and decided how to move forward each week. Now, I'm being accused of not asking for a delay on the project. All I did was ask for a delay on this project, but I didn't formally ask for them. I only requested them in our meetings and documented them in the meeting minutes. But that's not good enough for Dick Little.

I put my head down in my hands and cry out loud. My whole body is shaking, and I make loud, gasping noises as I cry. I'm sure someone is going to hear me. I raise my head from my hands, look up, and see Buzz standing at my desk.

"Loretta, are you OK?" Buzz asks.

"No, I'm not. I just received a letter from Dick Little saying the committee is not paying any of the previously approved overtime because I never formally requested a delay," I say as I start crying again. "He is such a lying sack of shit."

Buzz walks around my desk, pulls me up, and holds me in his arms. I can't stop crying, but Buzz's arms around me calm my shaking.

"Let's go over to the club and get a drink. Bring the letter so that I can read it," Buzz says.

I grab my purse and the letter, and we walk out of the job-site office to the club trailers, with his arm around me the whole way. We walk in and sit down at a table, which is now happy hour, not lunch. Buzz orders us a drink.

"I've never had a drink in here before. I thought I was only allowed in the conference room for our meetings," I say.

"You aren't allowed in here, but since you are with me, we're good."

Our drinks arrive, and I have settled quite a bit. I take a sip of wine and hand Buzz the letter from Dick Little. Buzz reads it and acknowledges he's just trying to do his job.

"By lying to the contractors to approve overtime. If I would have known this, we wouldn't have spent a dime on overtime. I would have submitted formal delay requests, and the end would be the end date," I explain. "But he told me not to, and I came up with a different solution. Overtime. And we agreed that was the right solution." I take another sip of wine and say, "Do the other committee members know he was going to send this letter?" I ask.

"I'm not sure. I know the committee can't do a lot about his decision," Buzz says. "But shouldn't it be the committee's decision and not Dick Little's decision. It sounds like a lawyer wrote it. My company is not going to be pleased with me. I report to them every month on how we are progressing. They think we'll do OK on this job. But with this setback, we'll be lucky if we break even." I sigh.

"Do you want to go to dinner somewhere?" Buzz asks.

"No, I wouldn't be very good company, but thanks for comforting me."

Chapter 33

The phone rang early today, earlier than usual, at 8 a.m. on a Sunday.

"Hello?"

"Hi, Lolly, it's Trisha."

"Hi, is everything alright?" I ask.

T's mom had a celebration of life for her dad yesterday afternoon. It was just like a party, with lots of food and drinks and friends of T's mom and dad.

"I'm glad you came over yesterday. I'm happy I had someone to hang with other than my dad's business associates who I see at work all the time," T says.

"I told you I'd be there for you through this whole thing." I smile.

"Well, we have one last thing to do. My dad wanted to be buried at sea, just outside the Golden Gate Bridge, in the Pacific Ocean. My friend Tom said we could use Glen's boat to deliver the ashes. I want you to come with me. My sister is coming as well," T explains.

"When are you going to do this?" I ask.

"Today. Sorry for the short notice, but we wanted to wait until after the celebration of life to bury him at sea," T answers.

"Well, Tony is supposed to come over and watch football today, but I can ask him to come along," I say.

"Sure, it's a thirty-seven-foot sailboat. There is plenty of room on deck. We want to leave the yacht club at 11:30 a.m. and will probably take a couple of hours to sail under the Golden Gate from here. Coming back, with the wind, will be faster, so we should be back by 4 p.m.," T states.

"Good. I'll call Tony right now and tell him I'm going, but he can come along if he'd like. That way I can save him a trip across the bridge if he doesn't want to go," I say.

"The boat is docked in the guest berths at the club. The name of the boat is *Foghead*," T says. "See you around 11 a.m. I hope Tony can join us." And with that, she hangs up the phone.

I immediately call Tony. "Hello?"

"Hi, it's Loretta."

"Well, hi. What's up?" Tony asks.

"T called and asked if I would join her in sailing under the Golden Gate Bridge and burying her dad at sea. I can't say no. I told her I'd be there for her. So, do you want to go with me?" I ask.

"Yeah, it sounds like fun. I mean, you know what I mean, the sailing part," Tony says.

"Great. If you are here by 10:30 a.m., we can get to the yacht club by 11:00 a.m.

They want to leave at 11:30 a.m.," I say.

The Country Club

"Who are 'they'?" Tony asks.

"Tom, who races on the boat, asked the owner if we could use it for the day. Also, T, T's sister Bev, and the two of us. They call me Lolly, not Loretta," I explain.

"Why?"

"Because that's my nickname. You sure are asking a lot of questions. Just remember to bring a jacket and don't wear black soled shoes. You'll be fine. See you at 10:30 a.m.," I say as I hang up the phone to get ready to go.

Tony knocks on the door at exactly 10:30 a.m. I open the door. He walks in and kisses me very slowly, and my knees begin to buckle.

"That was nice." I smile. "How are you? I haven't seen you in a couple of days." "I'm fine, the restaurant is fine, the family is fine, and I'm excited to go sailing," Tony says.

"Do you get seasick?" I ask.

"No. I've been fishing in the ocean, just outside the gate, but not sailing," Tony states.

"I have some Dramamine and am going to take one, just to be sure. The water just outside the gate is where the bay meets the ocean, and it's really choppy. We used to call it the potato patch. We better go. Are you ready?" I ask.

Tony walks up to me and plants another kiss on me. "I'm not sure if I'm going to be able to do this in the company of your friends," Tony worries.

"You can kiss me anytime you'd like."

I grab my Patagonia jacket and head to the car. We drive to the East Marin Yacht Club. We pull into the club and park. Tony picks up his jacket out of the car, and we walk to the guest berths. The wind has a chill to it, so both of us put on our jackets.

"Nice jackets, you two. You look like twins," T says. "Welcome aboard."

Tony and I look at each other and realize we have the same exact jackets. We climb aboard. I give T a hug. Tony gives her a hug as well.

"Sorry about your dad," Tony says.

"He's coming sailing with us today." T smiles. "I'm glad you two can join us. Do you want a beer? I brought sandwiches for lunch," T says.

"I'll take a beer," I say.

"If Loretta is having one, I'll have one too," Tony says. "You call her Loretta and not Lolly?" T laughs.

Tony just looks at her and smiles with those big blue eyes, which are going to shine when we are on the water. T calls to Tom, who is below checking the sails and gear, to bring up three beers.

"I'm celebrating the last sail with my dad, so I'm going to have a beer too," T says. "We used to sail together a lot when I was growing up. My sister and brother always seemed to have other things to do when we went sailing. I even lived on his boat for a while," T says.

Speaking of sisters, Bev just walked up.

"Hi, Bev. Come aboard, mate," T says.

"How do I get on this thing?" Bev says.

T just rolls her eyes and offers her a hand.

Tom comes up from below with his hands full. "Hi, Lolly."

"Hi, Tom. Long time, no see," I say, as he hands me a beer. "This is Tony Bertelli." He walks over to Tony, and they shake hands, and Tom gives him a beer.

"Have you ever been to Bertelli's in Larkspur?" I ask Tom.

"Many times. It's a great place. I live in Marin, so I go there often," Tom says. "Tony is part owner of the place, with his family," I explain.

Tom smiles at him and gives him a thumbs-up as Bev slowly makes her way to the cockpit, where we are all sitting. She doesn't seem too sure of her footing.

"Hi, Lolly, and who is the handsome man you are sitting next to?" Bev asks. "Bev, this is Tony Bertelli," I say.

"Nice to meet you," Bev says. "How do you two know each other?"

"Tony works for the drywall company that is on my current project at the Golden Gate Country Club," I say.

Bev smiles and takes a seat in the cockpit. Tom asks if we are ready to set sail.

Everyone nods. T pulls the dock line off the cleats and walks toward the mast, ready to set the mainsail. We are not putting a jib up today, so we don't have to tack trying to go into the wind right out of the gate.

With Tom at the helm, we arrive at the Golden Gate Bridge at 1 p.m. Sailing under the bridge gives you a completely different perspective than driving over it. A tanker coming into the bay passes us on our way out. It's like sailing next to a moving building. We manage to get through the potato patch without harm; it can be dangerous. We continue into the Pacific Ocean for another thirty minutes. Tom slows the engine to an idle, and T lets the mainsail down to half-mast. The ocean swells are small, thank God, but the boat still bobs around. This is when, if you are going to get seasick, you get it while the boat is just bobbing in the water and not moving.

T goes down below to get her dad's ashes and more beer for everyone. Bev and T take a sip of beer and then ask Tony and I to hold them while they do the sprinkling. Dad is in a black plastic box.

"This is heavy," T says.

She removes the lid. Inside the box, the ashes are in a plastic bag. I thought it would be a little fancier.

Tom positions the boat so T and Bev are downwind. We wouldn't want Dad to blow back into the boat.

T looks at her sister and asks, "Are you ready?"

"Yes. Bye, Dad!" Bev cries.

"I love you!" T cries. "You will be exactly where you wanted to be. Goodbye."

T opens the plastic bag wide and folds it over the plastic box. With both of them holding the box of ashes over the side of the boat, they tilt it towards the water to get the ashes to scatter into the ocean. The first inch of Dad starts to fly into the waves, but after that, Dad seems to be stuck. They don't want to touch it, so they tip it over even more. Suddenly, the plastic bag, with the rest of Dad in it, comes out of the box all at once and splashes into the ocean.

T looks at me with wide eyes and says, "Oh well then…not what I was anticipating, but we did it!"

The Country Club

Tony and I hand the beers back to T and Bev.

"Cheers, let's eat!" I say, and we all bang our bottles together.

T goes below to get the sandwiches and the kite, or the spinnaker. After lunch, T hoists the kite. It goes up the mast all bunched together, and when it reaches the top, it pops open with a loud sound. It's a colorful, large sail, and it's beautiful. We'll sail much faster on the way home with the big sail up. I can immediately feel the boat accelerate.

When we get close to the yacht club, T goes to the foredeck and sits there, ready the collect the sail as fast as she can, as Tom releases the halyard. We motor the rest of the way into the dock. What a beautiful day on the bay. We all help clean up the boat, tying up the lines and getting all the empty bottles and garbage into the trash. It is 3 p.m.

"Bye, guys. Tony and I will take the trash to the club," I say.

T comes over and gives me a big hug and smiles. "Thanks to both of you for enjoying the afternoon with us."

"Does anyone want to go to the yacht club for a drink?" I ask. "Sure, we'll meet you there," T says.

Tony and I grab the trash and walk to the club and put the trash in the dumpster on the way. Tony turns to me and kisses me just before we get to the steps of the club.

"Thanks, Lolly. I had a terrific time, despite the circumstances." Tony smiles.

"You're welcome. You didn't say much, but I could see you just looking at the views and enjoying the sail." I smile.

We both got some sun on our faces. I couldn't see those blue eyes behind his Maui Jims all day. He finally took them off when we walked into the club. I smile when I see the blue eyes that I love. The bar is deserted. We start walking over when Charles comes out of the back room.

"Hi, Lolly. Sailing today?"

"Yes. How are you? This is Tony Bertelli," I say.

Charles comes over to Tony and shakes his hand. "Hi, I'm Charles. Welcome to the East Marin Yacht Club."

"Thanks. Nice to meet you," Tony says, just as T and Bev and Tom walk into the club.

"Hi, Charles!" T screams.

"Hi, Trisha. What brings you here today?"

"Didn't Lolly tell you? We dumped my dad's ashes in the ocean today, and we really did dump them." T smiles.

Charles laughs and asks for drink orders.

"Three Myers and O.J., one draft beer, and one red zinfandel," I say.

We all cheer one more time to celebrate the day.

Chapter 34

"Hi, everyone. Welcome. This is the last official committee meeting. Loretta, can you give us an update?" Buzz asks.

"Sure," I begin. "We only have ten working days until substantial completion. The good news is we only have finishing touches left: stenciling the wood beams in the dining room, installing the beer taps in the main bar, testing the kitchen equipment, and installing the restored light fixtures. The wood stairs in the main living room are complete, as well as the carpeting and wood floor. H&S is moving out of the job site office tomorrow, so we can complete the paint and carpet."

"Can you postpone the finishes in the president's room until after the move-in? I think we would feel more comfortable with someone here to help us after we move in," D says.

"I could certainly do that if you'd like. It would be easier for H&S. I'll check with the painter and carpet layers if that would be OK with them," I explain.

"What about the locker room?" Dick asks.

"They are essentially complete. You can see for yourself if you join the final members' tour this afternoon," I say. "D, do we have anyone signed up?"

"We have fifteen, so we can squeeze in a few more," D says.

"Perfect. Oh, I forgot one thing. The electrical distribution panel is 'en route,' but the actual delivery time is unknown due to weather in the Midwest. Since the committee refuses to pay for overtime, we may not complete on time," I explain.

"When did he tell you we aren't paying for overtime?" Dick says.

"Dick Little wrote me a nasty letter to tell me the committee rejected paying for all approved overtime because I never formally requested delay days. I didn't request them because it was decided to spend money on overtime for selected trades to make the end date.

"Dick, is this true?" Dick asks.

"Of course, it's true. It's right in H&S's contract, section 5.3.2," Dick Little states. "So, the committee didn't know about the letter?" I ask.

"*No,*" the remaining Dicks reply in unison.

"Well, H&S will not spend any more on overtime to complete the project on time.

I'll submit delay notices with the new completion date on them," I say. "You can't do that!" Dick Little screams.

"Dick, you can't have it both ways!" I scream.

"OK, enough!" Buzz screams. "Does anyone have anything else?"

The Country Club

"We should have a meeting on November 5th, one week from today, to understand where we are on a final inspection, move-in date, etc.," Dick states.

"Good idea. I'll see everyone next week," Buzz says.

I stay seated while all the Dicks leave, except Buzz. I just look at him and smile.

He just shakes his head. "It's almost over," Buzz says. "I'm gonna miss you. Do you want to go to dinner tonight?"

"Absolutely." *The most important thing I can do as a project manager is develop a relationship with the client.* I smile. "Are you coming on tour today?"

"No, I have a meeting, but I'll be done by 4 p.m. I'll come and pick you up," Buzz says

"OK, I'll bring my car up. See you at four," I say as I walk back to the job-site office.

I sit at my desk and call Cal.

"Hi, this is Cal."

"Hi, this is Loretta."

"Hi." Cal smiles. "What can I do for you?"

"I just got out of a committee meeting, and I told them the panel was 'en route.' Do you have a confirmed delivery date?" I ask.

"No, I don't," Cal says. "I guess the weather in the Midwest has been brutal, so it's delayed."

"I need to know the minute you find out, so I can submit a delay notice if I have to," I say.

"We can work overtime on the install," Cal says.

"No, we can't. They are not paying for any overtime, and I told them that H&S refuses to do it then," I explain.

"OK. Do you want to catch a pop after work today?" Cal asks.

"Sorry, I already have plans," I say. "But maybe later in the week?" "That will work. How about Thursday?" Cal asks.

"Perfect."

I wait outside the side door with my box of hard hats, which at this stage of the project, I might get objections, but it's still a construction site. By 1 p.m., the members stand around, and all the Dicks are here except Dick Little and Buzz.

"Hi everyone, grab a hard hat and let's go inside and start the tour," I announce. "The space is almost finished, so I don't need to explain what it's going to be; it's already done. So, I'll just pick a path to walk through. Please don't get far away from the crowd. Feel free to ask questions," I explain.

We start in the main entry and walk down the new wood staircase into the living room. I hear some oohs and aahs from the crowd. It is beautiful. We meander out of the living and into the main bar.

"Is this open?" someone asks.

"No, sir," I say.

It looks ready to open. We go into the kitchen and then into the main dining room. They all look at the beam stenciling still being painted. We walk down to the men's locker room, and the oohs and agars start again. This is like night and day compared to what they used to have. They won't be bringing La-Z-Boys and microwaves to this locker room. We make our way to the lower lobby and bar and then back up the steps to the front of the clubhouse.

"Well, that's the tour. Hope you enjoyed it. Please put your hard hat back in the big box and have a nice day," I say.

"Nice job, Loretta," Dick the engineer says.

"Thanks," I say.

I walk back to the job site, and Cal is waiting for me. I am mesmerized again. "Hi, Cal." I smile.

"Hi, Loretta. I just found out the panel will be here November 4th, and getting the panel installed and inspected before November 8th will be impossible without overtime," Cal explains.

"Well, they have to lay in the bed they made," I state. "So, without overtime, when will the install and inspection take place?"

"With a week to install and another day to get the final from the electrical inspector, it puts us at November 12th," Cal says.

"OK. I'll submit a delay claim for our calendar days with a new completion date of November 12th. Thanks, Cal. See you on Thursday," I say.

"I'm looking forward to it," Cal says as he walks out of the office.

It's 3 p.m. I create a delay notice requesting four days' delay and fax it to Dick Little. I immediately get a response rejecting my request. I have had enough for one day, so I pack up the office, walk down to my car, and drive it back to the clubhouse. As soon as I park, Buzz pulls his car up.

"Hi, where do you want to go?"

"How about the downtown club?" Buzz asks.

"Are women allowed in there?" I ask, thinking of the only time I've been there.

"Yes, women are allowed in the dining room, plus you're with me," Buzz says.

"I think I should drive myself, that way we don't have to come way back here tonight."

"Just follow me. I'll tell them to save two parking spaces just outside for us," Buzz says.

"I'm following," I say.

We head out of the country club, and Buzz leads the way to The City Club. When we arrive, we find two parking places right in front of the front door. We both get out of our cars. Buzz makes his way over to me and kisses me. I smile at him, and we hold hands until we get to the front door, and then I'm on my own, I guess. He doesn't want the employees to see him holding hands with a girl. Heaven forbid.

We got seated immediately, although there were members waiting to be seated. We order drinks, and they arrive instantly.

"So, how was the golf vacation in Arizona?" I ask. "We really haven't talked since you got back."

"I had a great time. I just love those guys. We've been doing this for ten years now, and it's always fun," Buzz says. "Did you look at the menu?"

"Yes, I'll have veal piccata."

"OK. How's your wine?" Buzz asks.

"Tastes good to me," I say.

Buzz gets up and goes over to talk to the waiters. I look around the dining room and see Harry Henderson

The Country Club

and his wife dining as well. I'm thinking I should go and say hi. I walk over to their table.

"Hi, Loretta, what brings you to The City Club for dinner?" Harry asks.

"Hi, Harry. I am here with the general manager of the club." *The most important thing you can do as a project manager is to develop a relationship with the client.*

"We are finishing the renovation of the country club in a few weeks," I say. "Nice to see both of you."

I walk back to the table, and Buzz asks, "Who were you talking to?"

"The president of H&S, Harry Henderson, and his wife," I say. "Have you ever met him?"

"No."

"Do you want me to introduce you since we are renovating the country club?" I ask. "Yes, I'd like that," Buzz says.

We both get up from our table and walk over to the Hendersons' table.

"Hi, Harry. I'm sorry if I'm interrupting. I came back to introduce you to the General Manager of the Golden Gate Town and Country Club, Dick Buzzy," I say.

Harry stands and shakes Buzz's hand. "It's a pleasure to meet you. Has Loretta served you well on the project?" Harry asks.

"She has been wonderful to work with. Very knowledgeable about the work and aware of the activities surrounding the club," Buzz says.

Harry smiles and looks at me, and I smile back. We excuse ourselves to our table and settle in.

"Thanks for the great review," I say.

"It's true, kid. You've done a fantastic job dodging bullets from the committee and somehow getting the job to the finish line, despite Dick Little."

Chapter 35

It's Halloween, with officially eight working days until completion, but I know that's not going to happen. But the other trades don't need to know that. They can keep flooding the site with manpower to finish on time. If the electricians are the only trade still working, H&S can move all the tools and other crap out of the office. I'll keep working here after the move-in if it makes them happy.

The phone rings.

"Hi, this is Loretta."

"Hi, this is Tony."

"Well, hi! What's going on? Do you have a new project to work on?" I ask.

"Yes, I'm working in the Presidio at the officer's club. Guess they got word that Hard Drywall did the Golden Gate Country Club and hired us," Tony says.

"That's great."

"But I'm calling to invite you to dinner tomorrow night at the restaurant with my family," Tony says. "My mom and dad, sisters, brothers, and cousins will be there. They cook a huge pot of spaghetti and meatballs. Want to come with me?" Tony asks.

"Oh my, this sounds like an annual event," I state.

"It is, but you will like my family. You like me, don't you?" "Of course, I like you." I smile. "I just don't want to intrude."

"Oh no, I'm going to enjoy introducing you to my family," Tony admits. "Just meet me at the restaurant between 4:00 p.m. and 4:30 p.m. Dinner is at five."

"OK," I say. *The most important thing I can do as a project manager is develop a relationship with the subcontractors.* "I will be coming from the job site, so I'll bring some better clothes to wear."

"You don't even have to do that," Tony says. "They'll love the way you are."

I wish he was here and not on the phone, so I could kiss him.

"I could kiss you right now, but I guess I'm going to have to wait until tomorrow," I say.

"Until tomorrow." Tony smiles and hangs up.

Wow. The whole Bertelli clan, all at once? I'll probably be nervous, but it will be OK.

Cal walks into the job-site office shortly after I hang up with Tony. I look at the clock, and it's already 3 p.m.

"Are you able to call it a day?" Cal asks.

"Yes. I need five minutes to pack up, and I have to get my car."

"I'll wait for you to pack up and take you down to your car," Cal says.

"Great," I say as I start putting my computer in its bag and gathering up some papers that I might work on later. *I don't think so.*

Cal opens the door of his truck, and I step in. He walks around the truck, opens the door, and jumps up into the truck. We drive down the driveway to my car.

"Thanks for the ride," I say as I hop out of the truck. "I'll follow you."

I put my computer and stuff in the trunk. I get in the Miata and wait for Cal to start. I follow. We both meet at the Harbor Bar parking lot, get out of our vehicles, and walk to the bar. Cal reaches out for my hand on the way.

We walk in. There are two seats at the bar, and we settle in.

Barry comes over.

"Hi, Loretta. The usual?"

"Yes, please," I say. "This is Cal. He'll have a…" I turn to have him finish the sentence.

"…an Anchor Steam."

"I'll be right back," Barry says.

"So, it is going to be a busy last week. I'm going to keep my desk in the job-site office until they move in, in case they need anything," I explain.

"So, you'll be here until the bitter end," Cal says.

"Yes, I will be," I say. "You may be the only trade on-site the last couple of days. We are in pretty good shape."

Barry delivers the drinks.

"Cheers, we almost made it," I say.

"So, what's your next project?" Cal asks.

"They aren't saying. Think they just want me to keep focused until the club moves in and is open for business," I explain. "So, what's your next project?" I ask.

"I'm on my way to Fresno. It's an eight-week project for us. I don't like the Central Valley. I prefer the Bay Area, but that's all we have right now. There's a lot of competition in the Bay Area," Cal explains.

"You're not leaving until our project is done, are you?" I ask.

"No, I told them I have to be here through the final electrical inspection," Cal says. "Thank God. Do you want another beer?" I ask.

"Yeah. I have to deliver some things from the small trailer at the site to the main yard. I'm keeping a desk there, as well, until the bitter end."

Barry responds to the arm loop gesture for another round of drinks.

"Thanks, Barry. I'll take the tab," I ask.

"No, I'll get this," Cal says. "We may be here a lot in the next week."

Cal pays the tab, and we walk to our vehicles. "I like you, Loretta, but I'm off to Fresno, and I'm not going to get to see you after that. Let's just enjoy the time together," Cal says.

"Sounds good to me. I think we may need each other in the last week of the project, just to keep our sanity," I explain.

Cal kisses me softly. I get in my car and drive to East Marin. I stop at T's, and she's home. I haven't seen her since we went sailing to scatter her dad's ashes. I knock on the door. T opens it.

"Hi, whatcha doin'?"

T walks out and hugs me. "Come on in. I've missed you," T says.

"Have any wine open?" I ask.

"Oh, yeah. Do you want red?"

"Yes, that would be perfect."

T gets a glass and pours some wine for me. She already has a full glass.

"So, I'm glad you and Tony came with us on Sunday. Tony seemed to enjoy the sail."

"He's a great guy, and he really enjoyed the time on the Bay," I say. "Where were you tonight?" T asks.

"I went for drinks with the electrical foreman named Cal. I think you'd like him," I say.

"Why?"

"He is tall, tan, blond, and single. I'm just mesmerized by him. I need to introduce you to him," I say.

"So, when's that going to happen?" T asks.

"Well, that's the problem. He's moving to Fresno, and we only have a week to plan a meeting, but we can figure it out. Are you OK?" I ask.

"Work is good, and I'd really like to meet this Cal guy," T says.

"Your wish is my command."

Chapter 36

Friday marks a week left of this project. There are roughly 150 workers on the job, doing anything and everything. Some are demobilizing what they had on-site for the last eight months; some are ramping up and hitting it hard to get across the finish line.

Buzz walks into the job site office.

"How's things going?"

"Fine. Lots of guys here today, but I think we're in good shape," I say. "No need to work on the weekend. Dick the architect will be here this afternoon to start a punch list. Hopefully he can get the list to me by Monday morning, and we will have a whole week to complete it. It's hard to plan the trades when you don't know what's on the list."

"Do you want to go to lunch today?" Buzz asks.

"Sure, but I can't go far," I say. "There's too much going on to vacate the premises."

"That's fine. We can just eat at the trailer clubhouse," Buzz says.

"Perfect."

"I'll be back at 11:45 a.m., and we can walk over together."

I smile as Buzz turns and walks out of the job-site office.

The phone rings.

"Hi, this is Loretta."

"Hi, this is Tony. I'm just checking in to see if you are still on board for this evening's dinner with my family."

"I'm in. I should be there by 4:30.p.m.," I say.

"OK, I'm just nervous, like you're going to cancel," Tony admits.

"Honey, I'm not going to cancel on an amazing event like tonight. I'm really looking forward to it," I explain.

"OK, I'll see you at 4:30 p.m."

Buzz walks into the job-site office at 11:45 p.m. exactly. "Are you ready to go, kid?"

"Yes. Let me grab my purse."

We walk out of the job-site office and across the circular drive to the clubhouse trailers. Buzz opens the door and lets me in. He follows and moves forward to get the attention of the help. Someone sees him and races over. We are seated immediately.

"Can I get you both something to drink?"

"We want a red zinfandel, and I'll take a screwdriver," Buzz says. "And some menus."

"Yes, sir."

"So, do you have another project to go to after this?" Buzz asks.

"No, I was told to stay here and keep everyone happy, even if it's well after the grand opening," I say.

"That sounds good to me."

"Can I apply for a job?" Buzz laughs.

We order our lunch of two soups and sandwiches, beef with barley and ham and swiss. The soup is fantastic, and the sandwich is perfect. We finish up and walk back to the job-site office.

"Thanks, Buzz," I say.

He looks at me like he wants to kiss me but is concerned about where we are. I take his hand and lead him into the closet outside the job-site office door. I shut the door and pull him close. He kisses me like he has never done before.

"Thank you, Loretta," Buzz says as we make our way out of the closet and back to reality.

At 2:30 p.m., I take a final walk through the site. A lot of work is going on. It's impressive. I return to the job-site office and start to pack up to shut down. I look up and see Ben standing there.

"Wow, what are you doing here?"

"I thought I could catch you for drinks or dinner?" Ben explains. "Sorry, I have plans after work. How are you?"

"I'm fine. I have just been thinking about you, and I thought I'd stop by," Ben says. "You know you really should call before you show up like this," I state. "We're out of here in a week."

"What's next for you?" Ben asks.

"I don't know," I say. "I'll be here through the middle of November."

"OK, bye. We'll catch up soon," Ben says.

I continue to pack my stuff and close the office. I walk down to my Miata. I put my computer and other stuff in the trunk. I get in the car and start up the hill, out of the country club, to Bertelli's.

I pull into the parking lot at 4:20 p.m. I start walking to the restaurant, and I see Tony running out to meet me.

"Hi, Lolly. I'm so glad you're here." He kisses me.

"Hi, Tony. I'm glad to be here too," I say.

"Everyone is here. Are you ready to meet my family?" Tony asks.

"I think so. I should be fine," I say. *He is so excited.*

We walk into the restaurant, and he goes straight to his mom and dad, sitting at his favorite table. His mom and dad call him Antonio.

"Hi Mom, hi Dad. This is Lolly," Tony says. "Lolly, this is Maria and Vinny, my mom and dad."

"It's nice to meet both of you," I say.

"Oh, I just love your name," Maria says. "Thank you. It's a nickname for Loretta."

"Do you work?" Vinny asks.

"Yes, I'm a project manager for a construction company. Tony's drywall company is on my project. That is how we met," I say.

"Hmm," Vinny says. "You two sit with us at this table."

"I'm going to introduce Lolly to the rest of the family," Tony says.

He grabs my hand, and we walk over to a table with six smiling people sitting there. I recognize Angelo.

"Lolly, these are my brothers and sister. You have met Angelo. Now meet Giorgio and Lola," Tony says. "This is Lolly."

"Hi," I say.

"And the other three sitting at the table are my cousins Rocco, Sofia, and Angelina.

My aunt Lucia and uncle Leo couldn't join us today," Tony explains. "Hi." I smile.

We turn and head back to Antonio's favorite table. We sit down. Mom and Dad are in a heated discussion about happy hour.

Tony looks at me. "What's your pleasure?"

As my heart skips a beat, I say, "I'll have a red zinfandel." Others are waiting on us since the family is here for dinner.

Roberto approaches the table. Maria and Vinny are still going strong. "Good evening, Antonio. And who is this lovely lady sitting next to you?"

"This is Lolly," Tony says. "She would like a glass of zinfandel, and I would like a Bud Light. Actually, we will take a bottle of zin, and I'll have a glass at dinner."

"Perfect. I'll be right back with your drinks," Roberto says.

"So, Mom and Dad, what are you arguing about?" Tony asks.

"She thinks we should offer a happy hour menu that is less expensive than our regular menu to attract a younger crowd. I don't agree. The seniors come in early and pay full price," Vinny says.

The Country Club

Roberto brings the bottle of wine, two glasses, and a Bud Lite. He opens the bottle and pours a little into Tony's glass for his approval.

"It's fine," Tony says.

Roberto fills my glass and makes sure Maria and Vinny are good too. "So, Lolly, do you like spaghetti and meatballs?" Maria asks.

"It's my favorite."

"Well, you are in for a treat tonight," Maria says.

"I'm looking forward to it," I say.

"So, Mom, why do you want to add a happy hour menu to the restaurant?" Tony asks.

"Because I think the average age of our customers is seventy. I just think we could attract a younger clientele by having a happy hour menu that just offers a few things for a few dollars less. What do you think?" Maria asks.

"I sorta like the idea. To have only a limited number of items for happy hour, the regular menu still applies if that's what they want to order. There isn't anything to lose, only to gain customers and sales. What do you think, Dad?" Tony asks.

"I don't want this place to turn into the bar across the street," Vinny says.

"Think of it as customers who are around the age of Lolly and me, coming in, saving a few bucks on appetizers and drinks before they have dinner. That's just extra sales," Tony says. "I'll work something up and run it past you before I implement it."

Roberto returns with a big bowl of spaghetti and meatballs and puts it in the center of the table. Tony starts serving his mom, dad, and me. Roberto returns with freshly grated parmesan. The room fell silent as everyone began to eat. There are some other customers coming in. There is plenty of room for them since the family only took up two tables. The spaghetti is fabulous. Tony pours a glass of wine for him and another for me. What a great dinner. I love his family.

Once dinner ended, the entire family relaxed and enjoyed each other. "Where do you live, Lolly?" Maria asks.

"I live in East Marin, just over the bridge," I say.

"It's really nice, Mom. It has the most spectacular view," Tony says.

"So, you have been there?" Maria asks.

"Yes, Mom, I've been there," Tony admits.

I look at Tony and say, "Maybe I should go."

"I don't want you to go, but you do have to drive across the bridge. It was so nice having you here with me tonight," Tony says.

I look into his blue eyes and say, "It was incredible. Your family is great, and I'm glad I met them."

We stand up from the table and say goodbye to Maria and Vinny. We walk to the second table and say goodbye to everyone. Just before we get to the front door, everyone shouts out, "Goodbye, Lolly!" I almost started to cry; it was so touching. Tony grabs my hand and walks me to my car. He hugs me and slowly kisses me goodnight.

"Thanks for inviting me. I enjoyed myself. It was great to meet your family, especially your mom and dad," I say.

The Country Club

"I don't want you to go. Maybe you can come to my house," Tony says.

"You have to come with me if we are going to your house. I assume you want to catch up with your sister and cousins before you leave, so why don't you just kiss me goodnight and go in there and enjoy your family?" I suggest.

"OK," Tony says. "How about football at your house Sunday?"

"That will be perfect. You bring the beer, and I'll make some munchies for us."

Tony smiles and kisses me like he's never done before. I wake up from my trance and get in my car.

"See you Sunday."

Chapter 37

Saturday is a sunny and warm day for late October. I call T to see if she wants to come over and watch football tomorrow.

"Hi, this is Trisha."

"Hi, this is Lolly."

"Hi, how are you?"

"I'm great. I met most of Tony's family at dinner last night. How 'bout you?" I ask. "I'm fine. Not a lot going on, but I'm fine," T says.

"How about you come over and watch football tomorrow? Tony will be here, and I'm going to try and hook up with Cal, but I want to know if you were in before I call him," I explain.

"I'll be there. I like Tony," T says.

"So do I." I smile. "First game is at 10 a.m., so any time after that is good."

I pull out Cal's business card, which has his home phone on it. Maybe this will be awkward with Tony here, but I just need to explain the situation. I call the number for Cal.

"Hi, this is Cal."

"Hi, this is Loretta."

"Wow. Hi. I never thought you'd call me," Cal says, sounding flustered.

"Hi. I wanted to see if you want to come over and watch football tomorrow. I want to introduce you to a friend. I have a friend coming as well, so there will be four of us. Are you interested?" I ask.

"Well, I'm very interested in you, too, but it sounds like you already have a friend," Cal states, sounding a little disappointed.

"I think you might like Trisha. That's why I'm introducing you," I explain. "No strings attached, just a casual day of football, with some beers and munchies. What do you say?" I ask.

"I'm in," Cal says. "I'll be there at eleven-ish."

"Great. The address is 550 Viewpoint Drive in East Marin."

"Thanks, Loretta."

The next call is to Tony.

"Hi, this is Tony."

"Hi, this is Lolly."

"Hi. What are you doing?" Tony asks.

"Playing matchmaker," I say.

"What is that supposed to mean?"

"Well, I told T I'd introduce her to a guy on the job site. He's the electrical foreman. I had drinks with him once at the Harbor Bar. He is a nice guy," I say.

"Oh, you mean Cal? I know him, and he's a good guy," Tony says.

"So, you're not upset there will be four of us instead of just the two of us tomorrow?" I question.

"No, not at all. I like Trisha and think she might like Cal as well. I'll stop by the restaurant and pick up some fried calamari and bruschetta," Tony offers.

"Oh my, that would be perfect. Better than my chips and dip!" I smile.

I look at the clock, and it's 5:30 p.m. The house is clean, I had a big lunch, and I'm ready to relax. I jump in the convertible, put down the top, and head to the yacht club. I pull into the parking lot and notice I'm the only car there. I park and get out of the car. I walk up the steps to the back patio and open the door to the bar. Charles is watching the A's game on his secret TV behind the bar.

"Hi, Charles."

"LOLLY! How are you?"

"I'm fine. In one week, I'll be wrapped up at the country club, thank God," I say as I sit down on my favorite barstool. "Yes, please."

Charles pours me a glass of zinfandel, pours himself a draft beer, and comes to sit close to my seat, but behind the bar.

"So, tell me about Tony," Charles says. "He seemed like a nice guy."

"He is. He works as a foreman for a company called Hard Drywall, but he is part owner of Bertelli's in Larkspur. His family has the restaurant in downtown Larkspur and the retail store in Larkspur Landing. I was at dinner at Bertelli's last night and met his entire family." I smile. "Have you ever been to Bertelli's?"

"Yes, it's great. It's obviously a family-owned business because the kids sit at one and play with their toys while their mom and dad work the tables." Charles smiles.

"That's how Tony grew up, and he still calls it his favorite table."

"There is such a tradition there. I like that," Charles admits. "What's new with you?" I ask.

"So, Trisha had a good day on the water with her dad?" Charles asks.

"Yes, it was a good day, really good. Maybe I wanted it to go that way. So, you never answered my question. What's new with you? What's going on around here?"

"There is talk of installing TVs, and I'm just so against it. The only conversation customers have with bartenders in bars with TVs is 'Could you change the channel?' I'd never get to talk to and get to know anyone if we had TVs," Charles explains.

"I'm with you. No TVs. But Charles, you watch TV all the time, on your secret TV behind the bar, and that's OK?" I ask.

"Of course, it's OK," Charles says.

I smile and shake my head. "Are we playing dominos tonight?" I ask.

"Yes, 6:30 p.m."

"OK, good."

I order another wine; Charles gets the dominos from behind the bar.

"Is anyone else showing up tonight?" I ask.

"I think Gino will be here and Sammy."

I move to the table we play at, right next to the bar. Charles is technically still working. I dump the dominos from the box, turning all the tiles over to blank. Gino and Sammy walk in at the same time and sit down at the table.

"Hi, Lolly," Gino says.

"I'm glad you're here. Hi, Sammy." "Hi, Lolly," Sammy says.

Charles comes over to the table and makes sure everyone has drinks.

"Let's start. Everyone takes seven. We then pick one tile to see who goes first."

I pick double 6 and get the honors. I lay down the double fives and get 10 points. I follow with a blank five and get 10 more. I lay down a blank 8, so it's 18 to Charles. He plays a 5/2 and scores 10. Scores or doubles go again, so Charles plays a double two and then a 2/8, so it's 16 to Gino. Gino plays a 2/4, which scores 20. He continues with a double 4 and follows with a 4/7. Sammy plays a double 8 and follows with a 5 blank, for 31 to me. I have four dominos left. I play a blank 4, which scores 35. I follow up with a double 7, which gets me to 42. I play a 5/3, which scores 45. You can't go out and score. You'd have to pick a tile from the boneyard and play again. Lucky, I have an 8/2, play it on the double eights, and I'm out.

I win game one, Charles wins game two, and Gino wins game three.

"I'm outta here," I say. "Bye, Gino. Bye, Sammy. And bye, Charles."

I love playing dominos on Saturday night at the yacht club!

Chapter 38

It's Sunday, November 3rd, and the St. Louis Rams are playing the Pittsburgh Steelers at Three Rivers Stadium. I bought lots of beer and wine for the festivities. Tony, so graciously, said he would provide the appetizers. I'm ready for guests by 9:45 a.m. Tony is the first to arrive, hot pack in tow.

"Hi, Lolly. I missed you," he says as he gives me a big hug and kiss to start the day. "I'm so glad you came to dinner with my family on Friday."

"I loved it. Thanks for inviting me." "Where should I put this?" Tony asks.

"Put it on the stove. We'll keep it warm for a while, at least until the others show up," I reply.

Tony puts down the hot bag, walks into the living room, turns on the TV, and finds the game. There is a knock on the door. I open it to find T with her hands full.

"Hi, Lolly," T says as she hugs me. "I bought a bottle of wine and made some spinach artichoke dip. You can never have enough food or drink watching football."

Tony walks into the kitchen and gives T a big hug.

"Hi, Trisha," Tony says. "It's gonna be a fun afternoon." "What did you bring from the restaurant?" T asks. "Fried calamari and bruschetta," Tony says.

I put the dip and crackers T brought on the coffee table.

"What does everyone want to drink? It's only 10 a.m.," I mention.

"Do you have bloody Mary mix?" T asks.

"Yes, and more importantly, I have vodka," I say. "Tony?" "I'll just have a beer."

I get two glasses, fill them with ice, pour in the vodka and the tomato juice, then add a splash of Worcestershire, a dash of celery salt, a squeeze of lime, and Tobasco to taste. I'll skip that part. T might want some. And I even have pickled green beans as stir sticks. I hand T her drink and deliver Tony his beer. He smiles. Tony already has his seat picked out, and there is room for me right next to him. T makes her way to the living room and takes a seat, cocktail in hand. We start watching the game. The Steelers are winning ten to zero.

"Is Cal going to show up?" T asks.

"Yes, he said he'd come around eleven," I say. As soon as I am done talking, the doorbell rings.

"Why don't you answer it, Tony? I think that will make Cal more comfortable," I suggest.

"Sure," Tony says as he makes his way to the front door. He opens the door. "Hi, Cal, come on in," Tony says.

"Hi, Tony. I didn't know you are the 'friend' Loretta was talking about." Cal walks in and looks at the view of the city.

"Wow, what a view. Hi, Loretta. Thanks for inviting me," Cal says.

"I'm glad you can join us." T walks up behind me like she is in the sixth grade and ready to talk to the guy she has a crush on.

"Trisha, this is Cal," I say.

"Pleasure to meet you," Cal says.

"Nice to meet you," T says with the same mesmerized look I have when he's around.

"Why don't you go and make yourself comfortable. Cal, do you want something to drink?"

"I brought a six-pack of Anchor Steam. I'll have one."

I open a bottle and put the rest in the refrigerator. I walk over to Cal and hand him the beer. I look at Tony, but he's focused on the game. The kitchen is open to the living room and the view, so I can watch the game from the kitchen. I unpack Tony's hot pack. I put the calamari on a plate with the side of marinara sauce. I take half the bruschetta out of the bag, saving the rest for later. I carry both plates out with small paper plates, napkins, and toothpicks. It smells delicious.

"Thanks for bringing this," I say.

"My pleasure," Tony says.

He really likes the word pleasure.

We all finally sit down, help ourselves to some food, and watch a little football.

"Where do you live?" Cal asks T.

"Three doors up the street," T says.

"So, it has the same view as this?" Cal asks. He seems to be looking out the windows more than he's looking at the TV.

"Even better. Where do you live?" T asks.

"San Francisco, in the marina district," Cal says.

It's halftime, and the boys go out on the deck to enjoy the sunshine and the view. I get a bruschetta and some calamari with marinara sauce on my plate, plus some of T's dip and crackers. I'm set.

"So, what do you think?" I ask T.

"He's gorgeous." T smiles. "And he knows Tony. That's great."

"I didn't even realize they knew each other from the job site until yesterday," I say, as I dip calamari into the marinara sauce. It's so good.

"And he's a good guy. You both need to talk a little, get to know each other." The boys walk back in from the deck.

"Wow, this is a nice place, Loretta," Cal says as he smiles at T. "Can I get anyone more drinks?" I ask.

"Yes," Tony says.

"Yes," Cal says.

"Yes," T says.

I deliver the beers to the boys. I go to the kitchen and open a bottle of wine, pour two glasses, and deliver one of them to T. I snuggle next to Tony on the couch, and he puts his arm around me. The Steelers are winning, thirty-five to three.

"Did you ever go to Steelers games when you were growing up?" Tony asks.

"No, we couldn't afford to go to the games, and my dad worked at the University of Pittsburgh, so there were no business favors to take advantage of. But you get a sense of excellence, of perfection of the game after four Super Bowls," I say. "The town was totally into it. And then, when I moved to California, the 49ers won five Super Bowls. I was starting to get used to having a Super Bowl champ in the town I was living in."

Cal And T laugh.

"Did you grow up here?" I ask.

"No, I grew up in San Diego. My parents are still there. It's close enough to visit often; far enough to be on my own," Cal admits. "What about you, Trisha? Where did you grow up?"

"I grew up in Palo Alto," T says.

"Did your parents go to Stanford?" Cal asks.

"Oh, God no. They moved here from Connecticut, and my dad started a tech supply company. Lolly calls it Spacely Sprockets," she says.

The boys laugh. We turn our attention to the game. There are two minutes to go. St. Louis is on the twenty-five-yard line and ready to kick a field goal. It's good, and the score is now forty-two to six, in favor of Pittsburgh. I think the Steelers will win this one.

I reach for Tony and say, "Let's go outside and leave Cal and T alone." We get up, he gets another beer and another wine for me, and we retreat to the balcony.

"So, how do you know Loretta?" Cal asks.

"Sorry, I call her Lolly, and we met racing sailboats in the bay. We've lived in East Marin for a long time and have many friends here. Lolly is a good, true friend of mine," T says.

"That's so nice to hear." Cal smiles at T. "Would you like to go for drinks or dinner with me sometime?" Cal asks.

"Yes, that sounds perfect," T says.

"There is only one problem. I'm leaving for Fresno in roughly ten days. I'll be there for eight weeks," Cal states.

"Let's go out for drinks and dinner in the next ten days, and we'll see how it goes after that," T says.

Cal smiles, and so does T.

Tony and I walk back in and see the two of them smiling. I'm smiling because the Steelers won, and Tony is smiling because he's here.

"What can I get anyone? More bruschetta? Drinks?" I ask.

"I'll take another beer, and then I have had enough," Cal says.

Tony says the same as Cal.

"Do you want another glass of wine, T?" I ask.

"Yes. I don't have far to go. Just walk up the street," T says.

"I can give you a ride home if that's OK with you, Trisha," Cal says.

"Sounds fine," T says.

"There is more bruschetta if you want any," I say.

T and Cal walk into the kitchen and take one. They look at each other and smile again.

"We are going home," Cal says. "We had a great time. Thanks for introducing us."

Cal walks over. He hugs me and shakes Tony's hand. Tony hugs T, and T gives me a really big hug and says, "Thanks."

Cal and T walk out the front door, holding hands. I shut the door and sit down next to Tony.

"Hi, precious."

"Did you enjoy yourself today?" I ask.

"Yes, this is a very cozy place to watch football."

"Let's just sit and relax before we clean up. We can watch the sunset," I say.

We both retreat to the patio, drinks in hand, and Tony looks at me with those big, blue eyes. We both take in the view.

"I think Cal really took to T, and visa versa," I say.

"I do, too," Tony says.

"Do you want to stay here tonight?" I ask.

"I really want to, but that will change the relationship we have going," Tony explains.

"In a good way or a bad way?" I ask.

"I think in a bad way. I really like you, Lolly, but I'm so paranoid about what you might want or need. I've been married before, and it wasn't a pleasant experience," Tony explains.

"I have an analogy that I'm a whole cake, and a man is just icing on the cake. Some women are missing a few pieces of the cake and looking to a man to fill those in for them. You are just the icing on my cake. I have no ulterior motives. I don't want anything from you but love, family, and companionship. I want someone to spend time with and have fun with. That's all. I don't want or need much. I'm not that complicated," I explain.

Tony reaches for me, runs his hand through my hair, and kisses me. "I don't think I've ever met anyone like you before."

"I told you, I'm not like most women."

"I'm beginning to believe that."

Chapter 39

It's Tuesday, November 5th, four days before the contractual completion date of November 8th. At the last committee meeting, we decided to meet today for one last time to talk about completion, moving, and, of course, the father-daughter dinner dance. I take a long walk through the clubhouse. I can call it a clubhouse and not a job site because we are almost there. I still wear my hardhat to set an example, but the place looks great. I'm proud to be in this position with four days left. If it wasn't for the electrical panel, we would have completed on time. Of course, the overtime that H&S is not being paid for is the reason we are in such good shape. Hence, my strategy.

I walk over to the temporary clubhouse for our meeting. I walk in, and I'm the first one there. Buzz soon follows. "Hi, kid." He smiles.

I smile back. All the Dicks arrive shortly after. I see one new face.

"Welcome, everyone, to the final, *final* committee meeting. I want to introduce everyone to Dick Roberts, the head of the father-daughter dinner dance committee. Loretta, can you give us an update?" Buzz says.

"Sure. Hi. The punch list was issued yesterday, so work to complete it will continue through the week. Thanks for issuing the punch list so quickly, Dick. The painters, millworkers, and electricians will be here all week. Final plumbing inspection is tomorrow. Final kitchen inspection is on Thursday. The electrical panel was delivered yesterday. Bill's last day will be Friday. The H&S job site will remain thru the 15th, as we agreed, and I will stay to make sure everything goes smooth for the move and opening," I state.

"How long will it take to install the electrical panel and get a final inspection?" Dick asks.

"The panel will be installed and inspected by November 12th," I say.

"That's not going to work if the dance is on the 10th," Dick says.

"What if you work overtime to complete?"

"We still are depending on the electrical inspector's schedule to get a final."

"So, what you're telling me is to get a tent," Dick says.

"Get the tent," I say.

Dick Roberts waves and walks out of the meeting.

"H&S will schedule a temporary certificate of occupancy inspection for Friday. If we pass, the club can start moving in, but you can't occupy or open the space until the electrical final on the 12th," I explain. "Does anyone have any questions?"

The Country Club

"So, we can plan a soft opening for the 13th or 14th, and if all goes well, open officially on the 15th?" D asks.

"I'll be here to make sure that can happen," I say. "Any other questions?"

The house is silent. "So, the last thing we need to do is all agree that the contractual end date is November 12th, even though Dick Little denied my request for a four-calendar day extension," I state.

"Why did you deny the request?" Dick asks.

"Because." Dick Little says.

"That's not an answer. To plan the moving and opening of this club, we need to have a date of completion. This is reality, not some clause in a contract," I explain. "Does everyone agree that November 12th is the new completion date for the project? Let's see hands."

I see four hands for November 12th. The sole jackass is Dick Little.

"November 12th it is. Now the club can start planning their move and opening," I say.

I look up at Buzz and smile. I'm exhausted.

"Thanks to everyone for serving on the committee. I'm sure you will have bragging rights when the club reopens," Buzz says.

All the Dicks stand and say goodbye to me, except Dick Little. I stay to talk to Buzz and D about the next steps.

"So, we're moving out of the trailers on the 13th, start deliveries to the club on the 13th, and the trailers get pulled out on the 14th," D says.

"You mentioned a soft opening. I think that's a great idea, with limited press so the members don't show up," I say.

"Great point. I was thinking just a few supporters of the project, the committee, and other managers of the club. The staff can start getting familiar with their new home starting on Friday. Some things will be obvious, like food and drink. Others, not so obvious, like back-of-house management," D says.

"Perfect," I say.

"Are you OK with all of this?" I ask Buzz.

"You two are amazing. I'm good with all of it."

D gets up to leave and says he'll call and schedule a meeting later in the week. "Call if you have any questions," I say.

I stare at Buzz, and he is staring at me. I thought the meeting went better than I expected. I still don't have an approved delay, but the committee started to manage the project under my leadership, and that will take us to the finish line.

I get up to leave. "I'll see you tomorrow?" I ask.

"No, Thursday or Friday," Buzz says.

"OK," I say, and I walk out of the trailer.

I walk back to the job-site office, and Cal is talking to Bill about the panel install. "Hi, Loretta," Cal says.

"Do you two have the installation plan all figured out?" I ask. "Yes, we do," Bill says.

"Good, because I just committed to getting the final electrical inspection on November 12th. So, we must get there," I say.

The Country Club

It's 3 p.m. Bill says, "See you tomorrow," and walks out the door like he has every other day on the job.

Cal is still in the office, looking at me with a smile.

"Yes, I'm up for a pop today," I say.

"Good, I'll meet you at Harbor Bar at 4:30," Cal says as he walks out.

I lock up the office, take my computer and some files, and start walking down the drive. I hear a golf cart behind me. I look and see Buzz in the cart, and he asks if I want a ride.

"Sure, I'll take a ride." I jump in the cart, and we get to my car, and Buzz turns to me and kisses me. "What was that for?"

"You have led the committee the whole way, and I just want to thank you for that. I'm sure Dick Little will find it hard to get his next job. I'm not giving him a good recommendation."

I kiss Buzz goodbye and thank him for the ride, jump out of the cart and into my Miata. I drive to the Harbor Bar, park, get out of my car, and walk into the bar.

Cal already has a glass of red zinfandel for me sitting on the bar. He looks at me as I walk over to him, and he smiles.

"Hi, Cal."

I hug him, but no kisses. I sit down next to him at the bar. "Now, you've got me figured out," I say.

"No, I just know what you drink," Cal says.

"So, just a little business. Are we still on for November 11th completions and a November 12th final?" I ask.

Cal says, "Absolutely."

"OK, so I can relax now. So, what did you think of Trisha?" I ask.

"I really like her. Thanks for introducing us. We are going to Trader Vic's for dinner on Friday." Cal smiles.

"When do you leave for Fresno?"

"In two weeks. They have a place for me to stay for eight weeks and a few other contacts for me to make once I'm down there," Cal explains.

"That's good, right?" I ask as I take a sip of wine.

"Yeah, it's all good," Cal says.

"I do like your attitude."

We wave Randy over for another round of drinks. Cal closes out the tab, so I don't have a chance to pay.

"We have a week to pull this off. I already told them to get a tent to have their father-daughter dinner dance. Maybe you can do the temporary electrical in the tent.

You'll have guys here, right?" I ask.

"Yeah, I'll have guys here, but I don't want to jeopardize our November 12th date," Cal says.

"I hear ya, but it could be some extra work for Sun Electric, and the client will appreciate the help. I mean, you're here, and they wouldn't have to call another electrician," I say. "I'll call D or Dick Roberts and ask if they need an electrician's help setting up the tent."

"Thanks, Lolly," Cal says.

"I'll call first thing in the morning and let you know," I say. "I was also thinking about the power being out when they install the new panel."

"Oh," Cal says.

"The kitchen is getting a final inspection on the 7th. Is that a problem?" I ask. "Temporary power will be on until the final cutover. The cutover to the new panel will take four hours on the 11th," Cal says.

"OK. I'll let the club know. They are planning a soft opening on the 13th, so this might affect them. Enough about work," I say. "So did Trisha suggest Trader Vic's, or did you?" I ask.

"She did and said the last time she was there, she got tanked on one hurricane drink, and she's looking forward to having another one," Cal says.

"You didn't spend the night last Sunday, did you?"

"No, I just met her. I drove her up the hill, kissed her goodbye, and drove home."

"I just figured I'd ask."

The next morning, I call Dick Roberts to see if they need some electrical assistance in setting up the tent. Dick told me they could use an electrician to prep for the event. I told him I'll have Cal call him. I call Cal and give him Dick Robert's phone number to coordinate the tent job.

Chapter 40

The inspector issued a temporary certificate of occupancy on Friday, November 8th. That means the plumbing and kitchen inspections passed. Let the move begin.

I call D to set up a meeting to talk about next week. We pick 2 p.m. today at the temporary clubhouse. Today is Bill's last day. He has his personal stuff in a box, and Bill sadly looks around like there isn't even anyone to say goodbye to. It was one of those kinds of projects in that Bill managed the subcontractors brilliantly but had little interaction with the committee. He should be happy about that. There are no subcontractors on site except for the electricians. The laborers are here doing a final clean.

"Thanks, Bill. It's been quite the ride, but we made it, plus or minus a few days." I smile.

He walks over to me and gives me a hug. "Thank you for dealing with the committee and buying everything I needed to build the job," Bill says. He picks up his box and heads out the door of the job-site office for the last time.

The Country Club

It's 1:50 p.m., so I walk over to the temporary clubhouse and into the conference room. To my surprise, I see D and Buzz. I smile when I walk in and take a seat.

"Hi, so I have good news and better news. Which do you want first?" I ask.

"The good news," D says.

"The good news is the electricians are on schedule for a Monday cutover and a Tuesday inspection."

"Well, that sounds like good news," Buzz says. "What's the better news?"

"We got a temporary certificate of occupancy, so the club can start moving in!" I say. "So, let's talk about how to get to a November 15th opening."

D has a schedule of how to move back into the kitchen and the bars. The locker rooms and bathrooms will have their own track of stocking paper and lotions. I state there will be a four-hour power outage on Monday morning, November 11th, for the cutover to the new electrical panel.

"So, plan accordingly," I say. "Do you need electrical help to demobilize the trailers?" I ask. "Cal will be here all week."

"No, we're covered on that one. The trailer rental company takes care of the electrical work," D says.

"So, what are we forgetting? D, do you have a menu for the soft opening?" I ask.

"No, but I can come up with one a simple one," D says. "Do you have invitations created?"

"No, but that won't take long," D says.

"They should probably be mailed tomorrow for the November 14th date. Buzz, can you think of anything?" I ask.

"I need to get with the marketing group and come up with grand opening information to give to the club members," Buzz says.

"It simplifies the matter since golf remained open while the clubhouse was under construction, so Wayne is good," I say.

"Yes, you are right. It's not like we are starting from scratch," D says.

"I think that should wrap up our meeting," I say. "I'll be here through the 15th. The office phone still works. Call if you need me."

D runs out to go to the next meeting. I sit there staring at Buzz. "Well, we made it."

"No, *you* made it, kid," Buzz says. "How about we go into the club and get a drink?"

"Perfect."

We both get up and walk into the dining and bar area of the temporary clubhouse.

As usual, I'm the only woman in the joint. We find a seat, and Buzz orders for us.

"I'm still so impressed with your ability to cut down the things to do, to make it manageable. That's a great quality you have," Buzz explains.

"Thanks." I smile.

He grabs my hand under the table and smiles at me.

The move took place all weekend long. I'm talking dishes, utensils, pots, pans, glassware, condiments, linens, chairs, tables, and barstools. On Monday morning,

The Country Club

the electrical crew shut down the power for the cutover to the new panel. All the staff was aware of the outage. At noon, the power came back on.

Cal walks into the job-site office an hour later and says, "We're done!"

I stand up from my desk, run over to Cal, and hug him.

"We did it," I say. "Actually, you did it."

Cal smiles. "The electrical inspector is scheduled for tomorrow at 10 a.m., and I think we'll pass with flying colors. Thanks for suggesting the temp electric for the tent. It was a very successful job for us."

"You're welcome."

The electrical inspector confirmed he would arrive at 10 a.m. It's 10 a.m. on November 12th, and he is here. In the meantime, the final cleaning is going on, and the staff is moving in. I decide to grab a vacuum and start vacuuming the carpet in the entry and wiping down the reception desk cabinet. I am on my hands and knees when Buzz walks in.

"Loretta, what are you doing down there?" Buzz asks.

"I'm just trying to take care of business," I say. "We are so close, and we only have two laborers on site, so I figured I'd help. Just don't tell the unions."

Buzz smiles and walks into the clubhouse to see how everything else is going. The kitchen, bar, and restaurant are in good shape for a November 14th soft opening. Furniture for the restaurant, living room, and bars have started to arrive.

Buzz pokes his head into the reception area and says, "Do you have a minute to come with me?"

"Sure," I say as I get up from the floor.

Buzz grabs my hand, and we walk through the living room to the main bar.

"They need someone to test the beer taps. I thought this would be the perfect job for the two of us. So, I volunteered for the position."

I laugh. We go behind the huge bar and grab a stack of plastic glasses. They have ten beers on tap. The kegs and lines were installed yesterday. Buzz and I start on the left. The first tap is Bud light. Works fine. The second tap is Stella. We take a sip. Works fine. The third tap is Corona. It sputtered beer all over the place. The fourth tap is Heineken. It works just fine, and we take a sip. The fifth tap is Anchor Steam. Works fine; we take a sip. The sixth tap is Guinness. It works, and I don't even sip. It's too dark for me. The seventh tap is Coors. Tap works, and we enjoy a sip. The eighth tap is Lagunitas. Tap works. Sip is yummy. The ninth tap is Budweiser. Tap foams up at the pour. The tenth tap is Miller Lite. Tap works. Sip is good.

Buzz goes and tells the bar manager the third and the ninth need work.

"Thanks, Buzz, that was fun." I smile. I turn to the reception area, only to find the vacuum gone. The laborers must have taken it so I wouldn't do any more work. I'm just trying to help. I go back to the job-site office. The painters have started to prep the space for painting. My desk, sitting in the middle of the room, with a small table for the printer next to it, hardly distracts the work. I call Tony.

"Hi, this is Tony."

"Hi, this is Lolly.

"Wow, I was just thinking about calling you. How are you?"

"I'm good. The project is good. We got the final electrical inspection this morning, so now it's just move-in and opening. Can I buy you a drink today after work?" I ask.

"That's what I was thinking about too."

"Are you at the officer's club in the Presidio?" I ask.

"Yes."

"Let's meet at a place called the Final Final, just on the edge of the Presidio," I suggest.

"I know exactly where it is. Does 4 p.m. work for you?" Tony asks. "Perfect."

I check with the laborer since Bill isn't here, just to make sure they have what they need and will return tomorrow. They should be finished by tomorrow. I pack my bag, walk out of the office, and start walking down the hill to the car. No one stops to pick me up. The project must be over. I jump into my car and drive to the Presidio, find a place to park, and walk to the Final Final. Tony is sitting at the bar. His blue eyes hit me as soon as I walk in. My heart drops, and I smile. He stands up and gives me the biggest hug that lasts a few minutes.

"I missed you," I say.

"Oh, you don't know how much I missed you," Tony says.

I smile and sit next to him at the bar. I love this place. It's been here for decades and is always a popular choice.

Tony looks at me with those baby blues and says, "What's your pleasure?" to which I crumble.

I gain my composure and say, "I'll have a glass of wine, zinfandel, if they've got it."

Tony calls the bartender and orders our drinks. "So, how is your project going?" I ask.

"Not good," Tony says. "We hit dry rot in the wall, just outside the kitchen, and it's a huge change order to the job. They are not happy, and as you know, the client makes it feel like it's your fault."

The drinks arrive, and we cheers just for the fact we got together.

"I know, it's like we make up change orders to make more money, and that is so not the case."

"And the clubhouse?" Tony asks.

"Got a TCO on Friday and a final inspection today, so they are moving in and planning a soft opening for November 14th."

"That's great. Congratulations, Lolly," he says, as we cheers again.

"Do you have dinner plans?" I ask.

"No, but we could probably figure something out," Tony says. "Now that I think of it, we could go to Bertelli's Market and get some food and go to my place and cook it."

"I'm up for that."

We finish our drinks, Tony pays the tab, and we walk out hand in hand. We get to my car, and Tony says, "I'll meet you at Larkspur Landing. The store is next to the brewpub."

I drive to Larkspur Landing shopping center and park in front of Bertelli's Market. I didn't see Tony, so I went in to look around. Wow, this place is amazing. Meats, salami, pasta, cheeses, bread, olive oils, and veggies to make any dinner fantastic.

Tony catches up to me and asks, "What's your pleasure?"

I melt again and say, "I'm very overwhelmed by this place. I think you should pick," I say.

"OK, I will," Tony says. "You can have a glass of wine while we wrap up our order."

"Perfect."

I sit there, sipping on wine, watching how this place operates. It's busy, and it's like a deli and a store. You can get food for take-out or buy cooked stuff to take home. Tony comes back with a big bag of stuff.

"Are you ready?"

"Yes," I say.

"Follow me," Tony says as he walks me to my car. "I'm only up the way; just follow me."

Tony gets into his truck, and I follow him out of the parking lot and into the hills of Marin. I pull behind Tony in his driveway. He jumps out and hurries to my car to help me out. What a gentleman. He gets the big bag out of his truck. I walk up to him and smile.

"You've never been here before."

He hugs me, kisses my forehead, and says, "It will be OK."

After walking in the front door, my first impression is that this is a bachelor's pad. There is no color, no decor, no real furniture. We make our way to the kitchen and open the bag. Tony bought olives, mozzarella, penne pasta, chicken, and marinara sauce.

"So, what are you going to make us with all of this?" I ask.

"I'm going to make chicken parmesan," Tony says. "Don't worry. It will taste fantastic."

I smile and roam around his apartment, looking at his treasures and history.

"I see a football trophy. Is that yours?" I ask.

"Yes. I was a football star in my high school years. That's how I met my ex-wife." "OK, we don't have to go there. Let's talk about something else."

"So, I'm cooking a marinara sauce with olives. The chicken is ready to go into the oven at 350 degrees," Tony says.

"I think you have it figured out. I'm not a very good cook."

"I learned how to cook at a very young age, by osmosis mostly. I watched what happened in the kitchen and listened to what they were doing," Tony explains.

He puts the chicken in the oven and the sauce on the stove. Tony walks over and hugs and kisses me. I can't argue with that.

"Can I set the table or open the wine?" I ask.

"You can set the table, but you don't know where anything is, so why don't I set the table and you open the wine?"

The Country Club

"OK," I say.

Tony hands me the corkscrew and the bottle of wine. It's a little tight, but I claim success. I look at him as he stirs the sauce. He is so focused that I almost don't want to interrupt him, but I do anyway.

"Wine glasses?" I ask.

He points to a cabinet adjacent to the fridge.

I stroll over, open the cabinet, and pick out two big glasses for dinner. I walk back to the bottle of wine and make a generous pour for each of us. I carry the glasses to the dining room table.

"Can I at least get the silverware and napkins?"

"The silverware is in the first drawer, next to the sink," Tony explains. "I'll get the silverware. How 'bout napkins?"

"Just use paper towels. It will be fine."

That's exactly what I would have said.

The timer is going off on the chicken. The penne is cooked and ready to drain. The sauce is hot.

"Do you want me to help you?"

"No, just go sit down. I'll have everything up in a minute."

That's restaurant talk.

I go into the dining room and sit down. I take a sip of wine. It's great. A minute later, Tony delivers two plates of chicken parmesan with penne pasta and marinara sauce, just like at the restaurant. "I'm impressed," I say.

"Enjoy," Tony says. "Thanks for opening the wine."

"You're welcome."

We both dig into what is the best chicken parmesan I have ever had. The pasta is done perfectly, and the marinara sauce is to die for. I take a sip of wine.

"Thanks, this is amazing."

Tony smiles as he finishes his dinner. I pour more wine into our glasses and sit back and relax. Tony gets up, clears the table, and sits back down.

He picks up his wine glass and says, "Cheers, welcome to my home."

I cheers to his glass of wine. We both stare at each other and smile again. Tony stands up and takes my hand. I stand up, and he leads me down the hallway to his bedroom.

He stops and says, "Are you OK with this?"

"Yes, I've been looking forward to this for a long time."

Tony looks at me, kisses me, and lays me down on the bed. He looks at me and says, "What's your pleasure?"

I melt into his arms, and we change our relationship forever.

Afterward, we lay side by side, holding hands, not saying a word. I wonder what has changed since he didn't want to change our relationship. Maybe it was being at his house without me asking him if he wanted to stay. I don't know, and it really doesn't matter.

"Do you want to stay?" Tony asks.

I look into those blue eyes and say, "Absolutely."

Chapter 41

It's Thursday, November 14th, and the soft opening is happening from 2 p.m. to 4 p.m. today. The clubhouse looks fabulous. They have valet parking when you arrive, the staff is suited up in uniforms, and I could smell good cooking the minute I walked into the place this morning. Even I am wearing a blazer for the occasion.

D walks into the job site office, or what's left of it.

"Hi, Loretta. Do you have a minute to go through some last-minute details?" D asks.

"Sure. Where do you want to meet?"

"We can meet here."

I grab a chair out of the closet, right outside the door. *I remember that closet.* D gets the chair brings it next to my desk, and sits down.

"I'm a bit overwhelmed right now. I'm not sure where to start," D says.

"Well, how about if I tell you I will do anything you need me to do before, during, and after the opening?"

"That helps, thanks," D sighs. "What I need you to do this morning is to help set up the buffet area. I'm short a few staff members, and that would really help."

"Not a problem. Just tell me who to talk to, to get direction," I say.

"So, the next thing is sort of like a favor, but I am wondering if you could be the concierge, the host, as people arrived. Buzz and I will be busy right up to 2 p.m., and I know there will be early birds attending. You know what direction to send the guests and can probably answer any questions they have. It's like you work here, Loretta!" D says.

"I can greet the guests," I say. "Do you want me up front at 1:45?"

"I think that will work," D says. "You can go check in with Holly to see what help she needs at the buffet."

"OK, but I do have a question for you. Do you know how the father-daughter dinner dance turned out?"

"It was great. The young girls loved the tent. I guess they thought it was like going to a wedding, and they loved it," D says.

D runs off, and I go to find Holly. She is in the kitchen prepping appetizers.

"Are you Holly?" I ask.

"Yes. You must be Loretta. Dick told me he got me some help. I need you to place the dishes and the silverware on the buffet table in the main bar for forty people. I need to stay in the kitchen, but if you can prepare the buffet table, that would be great," Holly says.

"I just need a bit of direction, like is the table out there, do I need a tablecloth, and where do I find all the stuff that I need?" I ask.

"The table is out there. Come with me, and I'll show you where everything else is that you need," Holly says. "And keep all the plates and napkins to the left side of the table. We'll put the food on the right, with a huge centerpiece in the middle."

I follow Holly to a closet, just outside the kitchen, that has tablecloths, napkins, silverware, and plates.

"This will work. I don't do this for a living, so how I choose to arrange the table is up to my discretion? And what about a tablecloth?"

"No tablecloth. The table is a beautiful work, and yes, whatever you do will be fine at this point," Holly says as she walks away.

After two hours of moving napkins, silverware, and plates to the main bar, I decide I'm glad I don't do this for a living.

I find Holly to see if she approves of my work.

"It's great. Thank you very much," Holly says.

"You're welcome."

I walk back to the job-site office. It's 12 p.m., so at 1:45, I'll go to the front entry and welcome guests. I shut down my computer and lock the office. The painters should be finished by tomorrow, so that leaves the carpeting to be replaced next week. I walk up to the main entry, which is a four-foot-by-nine-foot door. I open it and put a stop on it, so it won't slam shut. I'm glad I wore a blazer. The first car to arrive is Dick the architect. As he makes his way to the door, he sees me and smiles. "Hi, Loretta. Great job."

"Just go through the living room to the main bar, which is where all the action is."

A few other members show up. I guide them in. The next to arrive is Harry Henderson, the president of H&S.

"Hi, Mr. Henderson," I say. "Welcome."

"Are you going to be host for a while?" Harry asks.

"I hope just another thirty minutes."

"Well, good. I'd like to buy you a beer if that would be OK."

"It would be perfect," I say.

The next guest is Dick the engineer, who is such a nice guy.

"Hi, Loretta. What a nice surprise to see you as the first thing we see as we walk into the opening."

"Thanks. I'm just trying to help where I can."

"That's nice. You've done that for the entire project. Thank you for your help," Dick the engineer says as he walks into the clubhouse.

It's 2:15 p.m., and the arrivals have slowed. But the next truck is from Hard Drywall, the company Tony works for. A guy gets out of his truck and walks up to me.

"You must be Loretta. Tony has told me a lot about you." "And you are?"

"Ray Smith, president of Hard Drywall."

I reach out and shake his hand. "Nice meeting you."

We both notice the next truck to pull into the valet is Tony. He gets out of his truck, smiles my way, walks up to me, and hugs me.

"Hi. I had no idea Hard Drywall was invited today."

"Me neither," I say as Tony shakes Ray's hand. "Ray asked if I wanted to come along since it was my project. Ray is a member here."

"I'll see you in a few minutes. I'm almost done out here."

Just as I am ready to walk into the clubhouse, Cal and another guy get out of Cal's truck.

"Hi, Lolly, it's good to see you. This is my boss, Bob Martin. This is Loretta Novak.

I call her Lolly."

"Hi, Lolly," Bob says.

"Nice to meet you, Bob. Enjoy. I'll catch up to you both later," I say as they enter the clubhouse.

At 2:30 p.m., I relinquish my position as host and join the party. The first person I want to find is Buzz. I see him at the far side of the bar and make my way over to him. I stop and get a beer along the way.

"Hi, I just want to say thanks."

"You're welcome," Buzz says. "Come with me so I can introduce you to a few people."

Buzz grabs my hand, and we weave through the crowd. We end up in a group of three guys.

"I want to introduce you guys to Loretta, the project manager on the renovation of the clubhouse. This is Dick, the accounting manager; Dick, the HR manager; and Dick, the member function coordinator."

"Hi, it's nice to meet all of you. The place looks fabulous."

"Enjoy, and I'll catch up to you later, Buzz."

There are a few other people I must see. I look for Harry first. He is at the appetizer table. He's talking to someone, so I say, "I don't mean to interrupt, but you did say you'd buy me a beer, so here I am."

Harry smiles and orders one up for me.

"Loretta, this is Barry Wise. He is the marketing director at H&S."

"Hi, I'm Loretta. Nice to meet you," I say as I extend my hand to him. After the politically correct length of time that there is no response, I drop my hand. Barry nods and doesn't say a word. And this is our marketing guy?

I roll my eyes and say to Harry, "I'm glad you came to see the project, and thanks for the beer."

I look up and see Tony and Ray bellied up to the bar and make my way there.

Tony sees me coming and smiles. I walk up and say, "So, how do you think this place turned out?"

Ray says, "It's beautiful. I just need to know when I can move into my locker." "Have you been downstairs to see the spa and lockers?" I ask.

"Can I go now?" Ray asks.

"Sure, if I take you. Tony can come along." This might be the last time I'm allowed in the men's locker room. "Let's go."

The three of us walk downstairs and enter the men's locker room. Ray is amazed how different it is from the old locker room. These lockers are stained wood, with benches in between. That's it—no drapes, no microwaves, no room for a La-Z-Boy. There may be some negative reaction, but I'm sure they anticipated that.

I look at Tony and ask, "Are you ready to go upstairs?"

"Yes, I'm ready," he says.

We all walk up to the main bar. I see Dick the engineer and go say hi. He seems pleased with the project. Ray and Tony go to get another beer. I see Cal at the other end of the bar. I walk up and say, "How are you? When are you leaving?"

"Sunday. I'm having dinner with Trisha tomorrow," Cal says.

"Great. Enjoy the opening." I smile and walk over to find Tony and Ray at the bar. Tony gives me a hug. "What was that for?"

"You look like you needed a hug," Tony says.

"Thanks, I think I did need that."

"When are you going to be done working?" Tony asks.

"I don't know. I told them I'd do whatever it takes, so here I sit. What do you have in mind?" I ask.

"I would like you to come over to my house."

"Oh, you would?" I smile.

"Yes, if that's OK with you," Tony says.

"I would be delighted to meet you at your house. We might want to figure something out for dinner," I say.

"How about pizza?" Tony says.

"Perfect. I like sausage and mushrooms."

"That's my favorite too," Tony says. "I'll call the restaurant, and we can pick it up when we get there."

The rest of the opening went well. People started leaving around 3:30 p.m. I find D and ask if he needs me to do anything else.

"No, you have done enough. Thanks for the help. It seems this was successful." D smiles.

"Are you opening tomorrow?" I ask.

"We can discuss it tomorrow after I talk to the staff and Buzz."

"OK. See you tomorrow," I say, and I walk toward the front door and run into Tony and Ray waiting for their trucks. "I'm officially off work, so I'll pack up and meet you at the restaurant at 4:30 p.m," I say.

"Perfect. See you there," Tony says.

"Are you two dating?" Ray asks.

"Yes, I really like Loretta. We're getting pretty serious," Tony says.

Does pretty serious mean you're sleeping together?

"That's great. Hard Drywall does a lot of work with H&S and has for many years.

They are all good people," Ray says.

Ray and Tony shake hands, and both give the parking ticket to the valet. I shake hands with Ray and go back to the job-site office and finally sit and relax. It's been a long day. I'm sure everyone is exhausted. I pack up my computer and walk down to my car. I hear a cart approaching, and it's Buzz.

"Get in, kid."

I jump into the cart, and he takes me to my car. I jump out, and Buzz says, "Not so fast. I need to say goodbye to you."

"Goodbye! Where are you going?" I ask.

"I accepted another job at a country club in Santa Fe, New Mexico. I'll stay for the opening but will be leaving next week. I wanted to catch you today because I won't be here tomorrow, and it's your last day here."

I tear up and fall into his arms.

"I'm going to miss you, kid. We've had a fun ten months." "So, this is it?" I ask.

"Yes, I'm afraid so," Buzz says.

I throw myself into his arms again and hold on like this is not it, but I know it is.

"I will never forget you, ever," he says, and he kisses me like it is our last kiss. I get out of the cart, and he drives away.

I get into my car and find a Kleenex to wipe my teary eyes. I'm a wreck, and now I'm going to meet Tony. I was not expecting that news today.

I leave the country club, drive across the Golden Gate Bridge, and arrive at Bertelli's a few minutes later. I walk in, and Maria and Vinny see me and run over to hug and greet me.

"How are you?" they ask in unison.

"I'm fine. Antonio and I are getting a pizza to go. Where is he?"

"He's making the pizza himself. He'll be out in a few minutes. Sit with us while you wait. Do you you want a glass of wine?" Maria asks.

"Sure. Are you both having one?" I ask.

"Yes," Vinny replies, and he waves Angelo over and requests three glasses of wine. "So, Antonio tells me the project you're on is over."

"Yes, the grand opening is this weekend," I say.

"So, what's your next project?" Maria asks.

"I can honestly tell you I don't know. This is the toughest thing after you finish a project, that you don't know what your next project is. But what's worse is having to start a new project before the last one is finished. You have no time to do either."

Angelo brings the glasses of wine and an appetizer for us.

I look around and say, "How's business?"

"It's good. Our regular customers keep us busy. It's the tourists and new customers that keep us on our toes," Vinny says.

"How's happy hour going?" I ask.

"It's fun. We are attracting a local group that is doing just want we want. Coming in for a drink and an appetizer for happy hour and then ordering off the full menu for dinner," Vinny says.

Tony walks out of the kitchen with a pizza box and a bottle of wine in hand and sits down next to me.

"Hi, I'm just chatting with your parents." "That's good. Are you ready to go?" Tony asks.

"Sure," I say as I finish my glass of wine, stand, and hug Maria and Vinny. "Bye, Mom. Bye, Dad," Tony says as we walk out of the restaurant. He puts the pizza and wine in his truck. He walks over to my car with me. He grabs me and kisses me. "I've been wanting to do this all day."

"Me too."

"Just follow me. We never went to the house from this direction," Tony says.

"OK."

I get in the Miata as he walks back to his truck. I pull out behind him, and we head into the hills of Larkspur. We get to his house, and I pull into the driveway behind his truck. He comes and opens the door of my car. He helps me out and goes back to get the pizza and wine. We both walk to the front door. He opens it, and we both walk in. His house seems familiar to me, even though I've only been there once. He puts the pizza on the counter and hands me the bottle of wine and the wine opener. Tony sets the table. I open the bottle of wine. I remember where the wine glasses are stored, so I get two out and deliver them to the table. I bring the bottle of wine to the table and pour two glasses of it. I sit down. Tony brings the pizza in with a utensil to serve it with. He sits down.

"Cheers," I say, as I raise my glass of wine.

We clink glasses, and both take a sip, and Tony cuts us both a piece of pizza. I hold my plate while he serves it. I grab his plate to get the piece he cut for himself. Maybe we are both hungry, but we haven't said a word to each other since we sat down for dinner.

"I love this pizza," I say.

"It's my favorite. Do you want another piece?" Tony asks.

"Yes, please."

After two pieces of pizza, I'm full and say, "I'm done."

I help myself to another glass of wine and pour Tony one as well. He has another piece of pizza, and I stare at him and smile.

"You like to cook, don't you?" I ask.

"In my own kitchen, but not at the restaurant," Tony explains. "I like making two or four plates of food, not fifty. I lose my passion for cooking when I cook fifty meals."

"I'm sure you do. That's like an assembly line," I say.

"Exactly. I like cooking for you." He grabs his glass and says, "Cheers to another dinner at my house."

I raise my glass. "Cheers."

"So, we can finish our wine in the living room, or I can think of something else we can do. What's your pleasure?" Tony asks.

I have to catch my breath every time he says that. "How about that 'something else' you mentioned?"

"I was hoping you'd say that."

Chapter 42

I am running a bit late on my last day at the clubhouse, but I don't have too much to do: make sure the laborers pick up my desk, table, and chair and take it to the yard—and anything else D wants or needs me to do. When I get to the country club, I'm waved into the parking lot adjacent to the clubhouse, so for the first time in ten months, I'm allowed to park up top. I walk into what's left of the job-site office. The painter is finishing his work today. I'll let D know when the carpet can be installed, hopefully next week.

D walks in and asks, "Do you have time to meet?"

"Sure. Where?" I ask.

"Just follow me."

We go into a small conference room off the kitchen. I walk in and see Dick Little sitting there.

"Dick is here because the committee is disputing his final invoice, and Dick is disputing the dispute. I thought you might be a separate view on some of the items to help get through this."

If D only knew some of the history between Dick Little and me.

"That's fine," I say.

"So, the first item is the new distribution panel. Dick is charging forty-nine hours for overseeing the installation of the new panel."

"Dick Little was never on-site during the installation," I state. "What about the inspection?"

"He was not here on November 12th for the final inspection," I say.

"So, Dick claims he was here for eight hours on November 12th."

"OK," D says.

"And what about the punch list? Dick is claiming eighty hours for the administration of the punch list."

"I don't know if Dick walked with the architect and engineer to create the punch list. They did it in a day, so eight hours might be appropriate. H&S received it on Monday, November 11th, and completed it by Friday, November 15th. At no time during that week was Dick Little involved," I state.

"Dick, do you have anything to say about Loretta's comments?" D asks. "No."

"OK, we will approve eight hours on the punch list, not eighty hours. We will deny the forty-eight hours for the installation and inspection of the new electrical panel," D says.

Dick Little gets up and walks out of the room without saying another word.

D looks at me and rolls his eyes.

"You've seen our pleasant little arguments at the committee meeting." "Yes, I have, but thanks for helping me out on this one," D says.

The Country Club

"You're welcome," I say. "I have three questions for you. Have you decided on a grand opening date?"

"Sunday, November 17th. The notice to the members went out this morning. There is no grand in the official opening. It's just you can come and use the club again."

"Question number two: Do you need me to help you with anything today? This is my last day on site. I'll have my desk and stuff out of the office this morning."

"Actually, I don't need you to do anything for us today. I have a number to reach you if I need to," D says.

"OK. My last question is, Buzz is leaving. I guess that's not a question, but I wanted to talk to you about it. It shocked the hell out of me," I say.

"It shocked me too. He told me and the committee on Tuesday. I take it he told you yesterday."

"Yes. I cried."

D smiles.

"He was a great boss and friend. He will be missed around here." "And are you trying for his job?" I ask.

"No way. Too political, and I like it out here at the country club," D says.

"I'll say goodbye to you now." I stand up and give him a hug. "Good luck on the opening, and call if you need anything."

"Thanks, Loretta. You've been a pleasure to work with," D says. I smile and walk out of the room.

When I walk back to the job-site office, the laborers have arrived and are moving me out. I grab my computer and purse and watch the rest get loaded on the truck. I look around and tear up. I'm done working here. I walk over to my car and drive home. I think I just want to be alone tonight, stare out the window, and wind down from this project, not just the day.

I wake up today, Saturday, November 16th, and I don't have to go to work, and I don't have a dinner date. I must clean my house and do laundry, but after that, I'm free.

I do my chores, and at about 1 p.m., I call T.

"Hi, this is Trisha."

"Hi, this is Lolly."

"Hi, what are you doing?"

"I'm calling to see if you want to go to the yacht club, just you and me. We can sit on the deck, look at the view, get a bottle of wine, and just talk. I need girl talk. I'm tired of boy talk."

"Sounds good to me."

"Do you want me to pick you up, or do you want to drive?" I ask.

"I'll drive myself. Last time what's his name showed up, and I left."

"Oh yeah, right, Ben," I say.

"How about 3 p.m.?"

"Perfect. Meet you there," T says.

I clean up and make my way to the yacht club. It's a beautiful, sunny day on the bay for November. I haven't heard from Tony, but I'm OK with that. He has a big family, and I'll call him tomorrow.

THE COUNTRY CLUB

I walk into the bar and see Charles sitting behind the bar. He smiles at me. I sit down in my seat at the bar.

"Hi, Charles. What's up?"

"I was wondering how you say 'what's up' in Spanish."

"Que pasa, I think. I'll have a zin, and Trisha is meeting me here."

Just as I say that, T walks in.

"Hi, Charles." T smiles. "I'll take a red wine as well."

"Do you just want to buy a bottle?" Charles asks.

"Sure. We are going out to the deck, so that will make it easier," I say.

Charles opens a bottle and hands us two glasses. I pick up the wine bottle, T gets the glasses, and we carry them out to the deck. It is 78 degrees, sunny, and not much wind. Fabulous. We pick our spot, sit down, and pour the wine.

"So, how was dinner last night?" I ask.

"It was great. He picked me up, and we went to Spanger's in Berkeley. The food was fantastic, and we had dessert as well," T says.

"So, did you talk about what you are going to do for the next eight weeks?"

"Sort of. We came back to my place and made love. It was outrageous," T says.

"*WHAT?*" I say.

"Yes, I'm so glad you introduced us. I really like him," T says.

"Well, it sounds like he really likes you too," I say.

"I think he does," T says.

"I knew it!" I reply as I pour us more wine.

T says, "So what about you?"

"Well, I don't even know where to start. So, Tuesday, November 12th, was a big day at the job site. We passed the final inspection. I met Tony at the Final Final in San Francisco, right next to the Presidio. Tony is working at the officer's club. We meet for a drink, and he suggests we go to his house for dinner. We get food at Bertelli's Market. You have to go there. It's in Larkspur Landing, right next to the brewpub. We go to his house, and we end up in bed."

"WHAT!" T screams.

"I know; I'm as surprised as you. I didn't think he wanted to go there, but I guess he did. He is a guy. I was at his house Thursday night, after the soft opening, as well."

"And…"

"We had fun together." I smile. "To think we both were not dating anyone earlier this year, and now we both have fabulous guys to hang out with."

"What about Ben?" T asks.

"Before I get to Ben, I need to tell you about Buzz." I pour more wine for both of us and say, "Buzz and I have probably been on twenty dates—lunch, dinner, golf. We have hugged and kissed, but nothing else. He's a great guy, and he always was behind me 100 percent at the job. He calls me kid. He found me walking to my car on Thursday, only to tell me he had accepted a job in Santa Fe, New Mexico, and this was goodbye."

"WHAT?"

The Country Club

"I lost it. I cried and jumped into his arms, but he said this is it and left. I'm still upset about it. I guess I didn't realize how close Buzz and I were. Therefore, I need a girls' afternoon out.

"So, when is Cal leaving?" I ask.

"We talked about this for a long time. He has an apartment in Fresno and asked if I wanted to come down there with him, to which I said, 'Fresno? You have got to be kidding me!'" I laugh. "Cal said he thought he should just have asked."

We both laughed.

"So, my suggestion was he give up his apartment in the city, and when he comes home on weekends, he stays with me," T says.

"Are you OK with him staying with you for a weekend?" I ask.

"Absolutely," T says.

"OK, well, it sounds like a plan to me."

I pour the last of the wine into our glasses.

"So, you still haven't given me an update on Ben," T says.

"No, I haven't, but I can. Ben and I haven't talked since I ran into him at Pub's Chop House. I was there with Buzz, and I introduced him to Ben. Ben was with a lady but didn't introduce her to us. It was the weirdest thing. And then a car crashed through the storefront of the place. Buzz and I were OK, but Ben came running up from wherever he was sitting to make sure I was OK. Buzz squared him up on that.

"Do you want one more glass of wine to watch the sunset?" I ask.

T says, "Sure, only one."

I go to the bar and get two more glasses of wine. I sit down with T, hand her the glass of wine, and say, "I love you. Thanks for being my best friend. Cheers!"

And T says, "Love you too. Cheers."

THE END

About the Author

C. Atkinson derived her pen name from her giving name, Charlene; her nickname, Cricket and her maiden name, Chopnak. Born and raised in a suburb of Pittsburgh, PA, she attended the University of Pittsburgh and received a degree in Civil Engineering. She was recruited out of college to work at a major construction company in San Francisco. She currently lives in Penngrove, CA, with her husband Kerry and cat Mango.

Made in the USA
Las Vegas, NV
27 December 2022